Death by Fire

DEATH BY FIRE

Anderson Reynolds

Jako Books

Published in the United States by Jako Books,
a subsidiary of Jako Productions.

First Jako Books Edition, January 2001

Cataloging-in-Publication Data
Reynolds, Anderson.
    Death by Fire / Anderson Reynolds – 1st ed.
    p. cm.
    LCCN: 00-134031
    ISBN: 0-9704432-1-8
    1. Mothers and sons–Saint Lucia–Fiction.
  2. Friendship–Saint Lucia–Fiction. 3. Saint Lucia–
  Fiction. 4. Domestic fiction, American–Saint Lucia.
  I. Title.

  PS3568.E8839D43 2001   813.6
                               QBI00-704

Printed in the United States of America

Death by Fire

Who told the French to move the capital from Soufrière, home of the gods of the land, to Carènage, a place the gods so despised? Now if the French had had the humility and wisdom to seek the Caribs' advice before moving the capital, the Caribs would have told them it wasn't by accident that the gods had chosen Soufrière for their home. The gods favored Soufrière because it was there that the gods entered their finest glory. The Caribs would not have failed to warn the French that the gods were jealous and vindictive gods and whoever crossed their path would bear their wrath in full. After all, the Caribs' very presence on the land was proof enough of the gods' vindictiveness. The Arawaks who occupied the land before the Caribs had dishonored the gods by planting cassava, their staple crop, on a patch of land the gods had set aside as holy, and had forbidden the Arawaks to walk on or cultivate. For punishment, the gods had sent the Caribs to kill and drive away the Arawaks from the face of the land. And if the Siboneys, the people who occupied the land before the Arawaks, could speak from the grave, they would have told the French that the gods had wiped them out with pestilence, after their *Caciques*, province chief, had blasphemed against the gods of the land by pronouncing himself God.

The French, the ultimate in culture and fashion, a highly civilized people, a Christian people, a colonial power, considered it beneath them to ask advice from whom to them were pagans, cannibals, savages. Besides, even if the Caribs had volunteered such counsel, the French would not have heeded their admonition. As civilized and Christian people, the French did not believe in pagan gods, the gods of the Caribs, the gods of the land. In fact, nothing could have dissuaded the French from moving the capital to Carènage. Not the boiling rage and rotten-egg fumes that shot out from between the breasts of the gods when the *Jako*, the messenger of the gods, brought news of the proposed capital change. Not the trembling fear of the Caribs as they came together, danced the dance of the gods, offered gifts, and sacrificed agouties in an attempt to placate the fury of the gods. Nothing. The French remained steadfast in their plan to move the capital. A veil of greed had clouded their vision, distorted their hearing, crippled their thinking, and fouled their spirit.

In those days gaining territory was one thing, holding onto it was another. So Carènage with its easily defended, deep-water, natural harbor was too big a temptation for the French to resist. It didn't matter that they had to fill in the swamp that formed most of Carènage before they could inhabit the place, and, even then, lack of natural drainage presented a constant threat of cholera outbreaks; or that the sea always threatened to swallow the land; or that the place was the hottest, most humid and least ventilated part of the island. Despite all this, in the year seventeen hundred and sixty-five, the French carried the capital to Carènage.

Stupefied with fright the Caribs cut their hair and scraped their bodies. Some jumped off cliffs into the sea. Some others walked for miles on their knees. And they all vowed to wipe out the French the same way they had wiped out the Arawaks.

The sores between the breasts of the gods boiled as never before, their smell was so strong that it drove fishes in the sea miles away from shore. And the gods pledged vengeance on the Caribs for not stopping the French, vengeance on the French for moving the capital, and vengeance on Carènage for welcoming the move so willingly.

Soon, the gods stopped protecting the Caribs. So despite the bravery and ferocity of the Caribs, through disease, enslavement and outright murder, the Europeans decimated them. And then the gods turned their vengeance on the French. The gods called forth no less than the English to wage war on the French. But the French were not easily denied. They fought so valiantly that though the gods were on the side of the English, it wasn't until 1803, after many battles, that the English were finally able to wrench the island from the hands of the French.

The gods also wanted to kick the French out of Martinique and Guadeloupe, but by then the French were too well established in these islands, so instead the gods of the land sent the *Jako* to ask Mount Pelèe, the goddess of Martinique, to do them a favor and destroy St. Pierre, then the capital of Martinique and one of the most prosperous of West Indian cities. This wasn't much of a favor for the goddess of Martinique to do for the gods of the land, because she too hated the French, with all their wine and smugness about their culture, language and religion. Mount Pelèe was happy to oblige. On May 8, 1902, it exploded with a force forty times more powerful than the bomb of Hiroshima, dislodging huge chunks of rocks, spitting liquid fire, spewing ashes and poisonous gases for miles into the surrounding area. In the aftermath of the eruption, twenty-nine thousand of the town's thirty thousand inhabitants lay dead.

But after all this, the gods of the land were yet appeased, their anger remained. So they turned their attention to Carènage. At first they were confused, because back in 1780, after the French witnessed the anger of the gods, the obliteration of the Caribs, to fool the gods they had changed the name of the capital from Carènage to Castries and had moved it a few miles south. But when the gods caught on, they reasoned that since they were formed by fire and brimstone, why not give Castries the same favor, but, only this time, it would be fires of destruction. Despite their anger, the gods smiled at the irony of their thoughts—what builds, destroys.

The inhabitants of Castries were far from amused. On the night of May 14, 1927, the gods of the land visited Castries with fire. The fire consumed seventeen city blocks, including the entire business sector. The whole town would have burnt down, but fortunately the gods of the sea took pity on the people, most of whom had nothing to do with moving the capital, and the sea stopped the fire. The gods left Castries furious, but there was nothing they could do. The sea was beyond their reach. So they bided their time, and on the night of June19, 1948, when the gods of the sea were away on vacation, the gods of the land poured vengeance on Castries as never seen before. Fire raged through Castries, burning to ashes four-fifths of the city. A young poet, upon walking the ruins of the city, coined the catastrophe "A City's Death by Fire." Even so, Castries had to consider itself lucky, because if not for the firefighting squad of the United States Air Force stationed at Vieux Fort the fire would have swallowed the whole city. This time the gods were more pleased with their work. But some anger still lingered. In 1951 the fire of the gods destroyed many residential houses on the Chaussee side of Castries, and on August 20, 1959, the gods burnt down St. Joseph's Convent, punishing the Roman Catholic nuns for encouraging the people to worship other gods besides them. The gods of the land were not only vindictive gods. They were also jealous gods.

1

September, 1955. Two women met in front of the Roman Catholic Boys' School on this first day of the school year. They exchanged greetings, quietly, and went their separate ways. The one called Felina, the one as black as charcoal, with natty hair too short for fingers to plait, and wearing black rubber boots reaching to her calves, and a stained, threadbare dress reaching to her boots, was on her way to her job as street janitor.

The other woman, the one called Christine, the one with *douglah* (mix of African and East Indian heritage) hair reaching to her lower back, copper-brown skin smooth as satin, wearing red high-heeled shoes and a purple dress—unseen anywhere else on the island—that clung to her body, mapping its geography in detail, headed to her receptionist job at a lawyer's office.

Unlike Felina, whom none of the army of school boys in blue shirts and grey short pants had given a second glance, an army of eyes followed Christine as she walked away with the poise and grace of someone who knew that the world was watching, judging, and admiring, and, left to her, would not be found wanting. All along the way eyes interrupted their business to follow Christine to work.

But what the woman did in the lawyer's office could hardly be called work, at least not in the eyes of Felina who spent her days picking up garbage, and, one night a week, joined the swarm of women in their banana loading odyssey. The lawyer as well as Christine knew that she was there for aesthetic reasons, like a painting, to provide a pleasing atmosphere. There was a second reason—the lawyer hoped to seduce her. Christine was quite aware of this second reason.

If Felina were to say to Christine, "what you do can't be called work, it is called prostitution," Christine might answer, "I am using what God gave me—looks and knowledge of men—to the best of my advantage."

By afternoon, when the sun had lost some of its heat, and the country folks had bought their supplies and had returned to their farms and villages, and the produce vendors that earlier crowded the market had closed shop, and the hustle and bustle of Castries had quieted down, the two women would head to the same community—the Conway. The two women occupied the same community, but lived different lives, and faced different destinies. Like this morning, their paths would cross many more times, but they would exchange nothing more than polite greetings.

Though the two women were never to become friends or to share the same destiny, unknowingly, they had brought together their sons who, beginning this very morning, on this very first day of the school year, would become inseparable friends, and would share a common destiny.

It wasn't for the sake of her oldest child, Robert, who was now seven, and two years into the RC Boys' School, that Felina had made the trip to school. Not even on Robert's first day of school, two years ago, had she bothered to take him to school. It had not occurred to her as it would to most other parents to take her first child to school on his first day of school. Instead, Robert had gone to school accompanied by some of the older boys in the neighborhood. But even at that tender age, Robert had not minded one bit. He had wasted no tears. The feelings between mother and son were mutual.

No. It was for the benefit of Ralph, her second child, that Felina had made the ten minute walk to school. Ralph had just turned five and it was his first day at the RC Boys' School.

Among the army of eyes that greeted Christine in front of the RC Boys' School, none did so as raptly as those belonging to Felina's son. His eyes remained glued on the copper-skin woman with *douglah* hair reaching to her lower back as she greeted his mother. He was too young to grasp the meaning of the slight sensation that developed in his pants as he gazed upon the beauty of the woman whose dress, seen nowhere else on the island, seemed melted into her skin. Instead he thought: I wish she was my mother. His attention on the woman in red, high-heeled shoes was so complete that he barely noticed the scared, five-year-old boy that explained the woman's presence. Only after the woman was out of sight did he take note of the timid boy who had inherited his mother's large brown eyes, copper skin, and Indian nose. In fact, it was this resemblance that made Robert transfer his rapt attention from the mother, now out of sight, to the son, and what compelled him to send a friendly smile to the sad boy standing alone amid an army of noisy school boys.

Robert, who was never known to direct a smile at his mother, or his brother, Ralph, and who behaved as if he were at war with them, ignored his brother and the noisy school yard, flashed a smile in the direction of the scared-looking boy, and moved toward him.

"Hey, my name is Robert. What's your name?"

"Trevor."

"First day of school, huh?"

"Yeah."

"Don worry, just stick by me, nobody going touch you. Last term some boy stole my marbles and I burst his head with my slate. Look, you see that boy over there with *jarry*, plastic sandals?

That's him. The lady that bring you to school, she your mother?"

"Yeah."

"Where you all live?"

"Conway."

"Yeah, you lying. How come I never see you? I from Conway too."

"Of course, that's where me and my mother live."

"I from Conway too," interrupted Ralph, who had trailed his brother.

"Go away, *salòp*, scum," shouted Robert.

"I will tell mama you calling me names," said Ralph as he shuffled away, sullenly.

The school bell rang and the newly formed friends separated.

Two months went by and to the exclusion of everyone else Robert and Trevor had become glued to each other. To Ralph's great consternation, they had become each other's shadow. Robert clung to Trevor because of his resemblance to the woman of copper-brown skin and hair to spare whom he wished was his mother, instead of the charcoal-black skin woman with hair too short for fingers to plait who had a hatred of him meant for another. Trevor clung to Robert to make up for the neglect of a mother he adored, a mother born with a love of men, and too occupied with life to bother much with the intricacies of raising a child.

At two o'clock on the last Wednesday of November, the inseparable friends were among the noisy crowd of school boys heading home from school. Ralph was trailing a few steps behind them. Robert didn't allow Ralph to join the conversation. He didn't even allow Ralph to walk alongside him and Trevor. The two friends were in need of no other shadow. Their friendship was complete.

"Let's go get shirley biscuits," said Robert.

"Where?" asked Trevor.

"At M&C," replied Robert.

"I don have money. You have money?"

"No, we don need money."

"So how we going get the biscuits?"

"Just come with me, I'll show you."

"You not going to steal, are you? Police will come put you in jail"

"Me, I eh scared of police. Just come, you'll see how to get the shirley biscuits."

So instead of heading for the Conway, Robert and Trevor made a detour and headed for M&C at the corner of Bridge Street and Micoud Street.

"Wait for me. Where you all going?" said Ralph, running up alongside Robert and Trevor. Enmeshed in each other they had forgotten about Ralph.

"Where you think you going? Go home, *lapocal*, penis skin," shouted Robert.

"I will tell Mama on you," Ralph cried, "I will tell Mama you curse me and you don let me walk with you, and you don come straight home from school. You'll see, you'll see."

"Go tell, *souse*, informant," said Robert. "What do I care? Both you and your mother can go to hell."

Unencumbered by Ralph, Robert and Trevor followed each other, in the heat of the afternoon, to M&C. The edges of their hair yellowish-red from sun exposure. A thin, white sheet of tiny salt crystals covered their foreheads and the sides of their faces.

They entered the store. Robert didn't go immediately to his target. Leading his friend, he circled one aisle, then another, all the while glancing around to make sure no one was paying them attention. Then he ambled toward the shelf containing the shirley biscuits. Casting furtive glances, he quickly stocked his pockets. Trevor stood pale and quiet watching his friend. Robert nudged him with his elbow, but Trevor remained motionless. He shoved packs of biscuits into Trevor's pockets and then led the way out.

Just as they were about to step out of the store, the store manager shouted, "hey, hold it there. What do you all have in your pockets?"

Robert bolted like a deer startled by a tiger, and the immediate thought of policemen and jail turned Trevor's timidity and inaction into flight. With some spectators shouting, "run boy, run," they ran, snaking through the crowd of shoppers, crossed Brazil Street, and found a dirt path passing through yards and between houses. As they ran, shirley biscuits dropped from their pockets. They continued running, without looking back, until they could no longer hear the voice of the city, until their tiny legs couldn't handle another stride, until their lungs felt like they were about to burst.

If they had looked back while running they might have realized there was no need to run so fast and so far, because the puffy store manager, weighed down by a beer belly, was in no condition or mood to give much of a chase in Castries' stifling heat and humidity. They ended up in a hillside gully that came alive when rain fell. Thinking that the whole city was on the lookout for them, they kept looking around. Trevor had done wet his pants.

"The police will come arrest us," said Trevor.

"Ah-ah," said Robert, "they don know where we is. You pee on you?"

"Ah-ah, is sweat I sweating."

"That eh no sweat, that's pee."

"You got any biscuits?" asked Robert.

"Nay, all drop out."

"Mine fell out too, I only got one."

They shared what remained of their catch and stayed put in the gulley, their eyes patrolling for danger. After a long while they dozed off. When they woke, it was five o'clock, and the sun had already lost most of its heat. Trevor's pants were almost dry.

"Do you think they still looking for us?" asked Trevor.

"No, the store already close. Everybody go home already."

They descended the hill, took Laborie Street, avoiding Bridge Street and M&C, and headed for the Conway. All along the way every policeman they saw was on the look out for them. Every shout or loud voice was saying, "there go the thieves. Arrest them! Arrest them!"

They kept their heads down, and made themselves as small as possible, not looking into the eyes of anyone they met. As they passed the market they didn't smell its decaying-meat stench. They didn't see the calm of the Caribbean Sea. They didn't hear the radios that were spilling the afternoon news out of the houses they passed. They didn't even feel their feet on the now cooling asphalt road. They were in the weightlessness of fear.

As if it would help, Trevor stuck as close to Robert as he could. It was as if he wanted to melt, to disappear, into his friend's body.

Trevor worried about jail and police, but Robert feared his mother. As they entered the narrow, urine-smelling walk paths of the Conway, Robert could picture Ralph gleefully telling on him, and his mother waiting, waiting for him. She was always happy to have an excuse to use the tamarind whip on him. This one would be a fresh whip—the fifth fresh whip in two weeks. She had broken the last whip on him two days ago when he stole Mrs. Cora Hutchinson's pennies to buy coconut tablets. The two pennies sitting lonely on Mrs. Hutchinson's sewing machine, begging to be taken, had been too big a temptation. But the mistake he had made was to share the tablets with Trevor to the exclusion of Ralph who had begged and cried for his share. As soon as they had arrived home from school, Ralph had promptly told on him. Robert's buttocks still remembered this last whipping. At all such beatings, he could sense, in the savageness of the lashes and the glare in her eyes, her hatred for him. But what he didn't know was that it was a misplaced hatred. It was a hatred meant for another.

When the inseparable friends came to a fork in the path, they split up. One with relief, the other with trepidation.

Robert entered the yard, nervously massaging his throat as if it were the source of his problems. He ducked under clothes drying on a line. A small gust lifted a wisp of ashes from a coalpot upon which sat a hissing kettle of water. Ralph was standing in the doorway on the lookout. As soon as he saw his brother, he went for his mother. He would not have to wait much longer for his revenge. Felina appeared at the door with the new tamarind whip in hand.

"Where you come from boy?" she asked.

"I was playing football," replied Robert. His toe digging into his *Bata*, canvas shoes, his eyes glued to the feet of his mother, his hands soothing his throat.

"Boy, look at me when I speaking to you, and move your hand from your throat. Now, I'm asking you for the last time, where you been?"

"I was playing football, Mama," said Robert, tearing his hand away from his throat, and forcing his eyes upward to greet his mother's anger, her hatred. His efforts produced only momentary results. His hand quickly returned to his throat and his eyes to the ground.

"He is lying, Mama. He and Trevor went into town," said Ralph.

"Shut up and let me do the talking," said Felina.

"So what were you and that *douglah* boy doing at M&C?"

"I didn't go there, Mama, I was playing football all the time."

She knew full well where he had been. Besides Ralph's report, her neighbor, Colletta, who saw herself as the guardian of the neighborhood, had told her she saw her son and the *douglah* boy, pockets stuffed with shirley biscuits, being chased by the manager of M&C. But even if no one had told her anything, as soon as she saw the boy's hand move to his throat, she knew he was lying. Still, she wanted to find out what kind of a lie the boy would make up this time. The lie would help her gather her anger, her misplaced hatred.

"Boy, don't I give you breakfast in the morning?"

"Yes, Mama."

"When school let go for lunch, don't you find your lunch waiting for you on the table?"

"Yes, Mama."

"Do I let you go to bed on an empty belly?"

"No, Mama."

"So tell me, why you had to shame me and go steal the people biscuit? Didn't just the other day I cut your backside when you stole Mrs. Hutchinson's pennies? And just the other day you bust a boy's head with your slate. And you always cursing and kicking your brother, but you treat that *douglah* boy like a little Jesus. So tell me, what am I to do with you? You want to do me like your father did me? And you are not only a thief, you are a goddamn liar. Bad as it is, I can stand a thief, but I just can't stand a liar. That was what your good for nothing father was—a goddamn liar. Like father, like son. Well, if it is the last thing I do, I'll get this lying out of you."

"Take off your clothes."

"Mama?"

"I said, take off your clothes. If you cursed, then I more cursed than you."

Crying, Robert began to slowly undress. He was moving too slowly for Felina. She grabbed and pulled him toward her. He struggled to get free. She slapped him into submission and stripped him naked. Then with her whip in hand she dragged him onto the walk path, in full view of the neighborhood. At whatever cost, she was going to exorcise the father out of the son.

The whip cut savagely across Robert's back. Each lash was an eternity of pain. Amid bawls of pain he begged for mercy.

"Mama, please, I eh go do it again. I promise, Mama, I promise."

But Felina didn't hear his cry. As in previous beatings, punishing the boy was tantamount to punishing the boy's father for betraying her love and dreams. Love and dreams that had since cemented into bitterness and hatred. A hatred, in the absence of the father, transferred to the son.

Colletta was at Cora checking on the church-dress that Cora was sewing for her when they heard Robert's mercy pleas like one about to be put to death. As they stepped out to witness once again Felina's whipping of her boy, Sophia who was passing by joined them.

Child-whipping was no news to Conway people. Every child got whipped. But Felina's whipping of her boy was different. Watching her whip her son was like watching someone in a trance. She became oblivious to the world. Her entire being seemed totally dedicated to each blow she struck. So her whippings had become a steady attraction and a ready conversation piece for her neighbors.

Bearing witness to Felina's mercilessness, the three women gave voice to their thoughts.

"Last week," explained Sophia, "I said to her, Felina, why you beat your boy so? One of these days you going to kill him, you know. You know what she told me? She said that I should go mind my own business. I too nosey." Sophia was twenty-five years old, same age as Felina. She had two children, one six and the other three. She was shacking up with the father of her two children, an auto-mechanic. Sophia was a Catholic but went to church only on special occasions—Easter Sunday, Christmas Eve, and when she christened her children.

"That Felina boy was born cursed," said Colletta. "I was there by M&C minding my business, when suddenly Felina's boy, followed by the *douglah* boy—what's his mother's name—that good-looking *douglah* woman, the one who won calypso queen sometime ago? Christine, yes Christine's boy, burst out of the store, with the fat M&C manager chasing them, shirley biscuits flying out of their pockets. That Felina boy is cursed if there ever was a child that was cursed. I have never seen a child take so much licks, and don't straighten out." Colletta was in her mid-fifties, married but childless. She spent her days at bus depots and at Clarke and Gaiety Cinema selling condiments from a large tray. Her husband was a bricklayer. Colletta was a devoted Catholic, she was married to the church.

"I don't know, Colletta, I don't know about him being cursed," said Cora. "God is not so cruel. That Felina beats the child as if she is possessed. The way she beats the child and always talking bad about his father, I would swear she hates the child. It is as if the child is to blame for his father's betrayal. She is taking it out on the poor child. What that child needs is caring and the love of Jesus." In her mid-thirties, Cora was married with six children. She was a seamstress and worked from her home. Her husband worked as a government clerk. Both were active members of the *Christ Is The Answer* Church.

"Believe me Cora, that boy is cursed," said Colletta."Isn't Felina from L'Abbaye, and don't you know L'Abbaye people curse? She is supposed to be Catholic but she never goes to church. Not even on Easter Sunday, or Christmas Eve. She didn't even christen her children, she just signed their names in the registry. That was it. No christening. Her children have yet to see the inside of a church."

"Colletta, the boy hasn't known the love of Jesus," said Cora. "God hasn't laid his merciful hands upon him."

"Once," said Colletta, "I tell Felina let's go to church. You know what she told me? She said, 'I and God have no business. What use is God if He is never around when you most need Him. He wasn't there twenty years ago when the landslide buried alive my father and brothers and sisters, and He didn't hear my prayers the night, thirteen years ago, my mother died in a pool of coughed-up blood. So tell me, of what use is such a God? No. I finish with God. He and I have no business.' This was what she told me, word for word. Lord, if I lying, strike me dead."

"My God! She said that in truth?" said Cora. "The woman

has forsaken God."

"So now you believe me when I tell you that L'Abbaye people curse. I tell you, there is a curse on that woman's family going way back to L'Abbaye. Did you know that Robert was born on no other day but the day Castries burned down. Yes, the child was born in the middle of the fire. But not only that, he was born with his umbilical cord wrapped around his neck. It was a miracle he didn't die. I tell you, there is a curse on these people."

"She needs Christ now more than ever," said Cora. "Nothing is too great for Christ to overcome."

"You could try, but I don't think that will do much good," said Colletta. "The woman has passed the point of no return. Who is cursed is cursed. End of story."

"But what landslide she talking about?" asked Sophia.

"Child, you mean to tell me you haven't heard about the 1938 landslide that killed over a hundred people at L'Abbaye and Ravine Poisson?" answered Colletta.

Deaf to her son's pleas of mercy and the neighbor's gossip, Felina whipped her son with unconscious passion. At the tenth lash, the whip broke. With the breaking of the whip, she kicked her son in the buttocks, knocking him to the dirt. Long before the last lash, Robert's urine of pain had soaked into Conway's pathway, joining those spurted by other inhabitants of Conway, though under more pleasant circumstances and less public scrutiny. Good thing he was naked; he need not worry about soiling his clothes. He lay in the dirt, sobbing.

"Get up, get up, *salòp*. Get up, go clean yourself," shouted Felina. She had worked up quite a sweat. Her misplaced hatred had obtained momentary relief.

Robert got up and ran into the house. He kept screaming, "I will tell my daddy, I will tell my daddy."

Felina laughed a disdainful laugh, a laugh of victory, a victory in an unseen war.

His body on fire, Robert didn't hear the laugh. He resolved

to search for his daddy. Under his veil of tears he was thinking: when I find my daddy, I will tell on her. I will tell him how she calls him a liar, a good for nothing. How she beats me for every little thing. How she don love me; it's Ralph, the *souse*, she loves. My daddy will burst her arse. She'll see, she'll see.

Upon entering the house, Robert came face to face with a smiling Ralph. He charged Ralph, kicking and cuffing him and shouting, "*souse, souse.*" Ralph's howl of pain made Felina come rushing in like a tigress springing in rescue of her cubs from hyenas. She flung Robert aside. Robert tumbled over a couple of chairs. Felina pulled him up and slapped him several times.

"Next time you lay hands on your brother, I going to cutoff your hands. I missed your father, but I eh go miss you," she shouted.

Long afterwards, when Felina was having trouble falling asleep, when her hatred and heart beat had quieted down, she was filled with pity and remorse. She resolved to keep her hatred in check, and start treating the boy with the same love and care that she treated her Ralph. After all, why should she make the boy pay for the wrongs of his father? By way of apology, in a soft voice she told the naked, whipped boy, "you should start listening to me, so I wouldn't have to beat you like this." But the boy didn't hear her, he wasn't in the same room with her. Besides, the damage had been done and the damage would continue being done.

At home Trevor faced a much less intense situation. An empty house greeted him. On the dining table were bread and cheese and a glass of juice so his belly need not stay as quiet as the house. Christine had arrived home and left. She had a rendezvous with a married man up the Morne. By now Trevor was well familiar with the routine. When, after school or out playing, he found the house empty of the mother he adored, the mother men were depriving him of, he was to eat and drink what was on the table and go to Mrs. Stephen, the next door neighbor, and play with her five children, one of whom was his age. While he played, he would keep hoping that his mother would come and get him any minute— the mother he thought was more lovely than angels and sweeter, at least when she was around, than guava jelly. Sometimes she did, that is, when she arrived before bedtime. But most times she returned in the small hours of the night and by then he was lost in sleep among Mrs. Stephen's children, like he was just another one of the litter. He yearned for any kind of attention from his mother. He would have preferred even the kind Robert received from Felina than this non-attention. Even when his mother was at home, the attention he received was minuscule. She was either too busy managing her beauty or entertaining men. Her two-bed-room house bought for her by Trevor's father in exchange for a sworn secrecy about Trevor's true parentage drew a non-ending stream of men. Most of them didn't get what was at the back of their minds. But they made do with a laugh full of promise, a smile meant just for them, an eyelid flutter telling them they were special. So with all these men vying for his mother's attention, preferring a laugh, a smile, an eyelid flutter, a promise of sex to certain sex from some other woman, Trevor couldn't compete. Not that he didn't try. When he dared interrupt the spellbound men's undivided attention to his mother with something like "Mama, today the teacher made us count from one to twenty," the silly, smiling eyes of the men who under his mother's spell had become boys looked at him but didn't see him. And his mother would respond, "Trevor, how many times have I told you not to interrupt when grownups are talking. Go out and play with Mrs. Stephen's children." He soon learned to keep quiet when his mother was entertaining and watch with envy the magic his mother spun over the men whose need of her seemed even stronger than his.

2

The year was 1938, the month was October, and it was the hurricane season. Prophets of doom riding horse-drawn carts with attached bells traversed the main roads passing through farming villages and all the streets of the towns lining the island's coast, shouting their warning of an upcoming hurricane. The people should stock their houses with food, hammers, nails, candles and kerosine lamps. And those whose houses were suspect should consider seeking refuge in Roman Catholic Churches, then the largest and most sturdy buildings on the island.

In more eloquent voices, at every hour of the day, the radio repeated, in both English and *Kwéyòl*, the message of impending disaster.

The warning cries of the prophets of doom and the eloquent voices on the radio were largely unnecessary. Even the tiniest creatures of the land could sense the danger. Nature had telecast its own mischief. For two days, dark, heavy clouds had blanketed the sun. The land had entered a perpetual predawn. The air was chilly, and, though rain was yet to fall, damp. The people could even smell the rain. With such potent signs of pending danger, the people stocked and reinforced their houses with more diligence than the criers of doom had advised. So when, on the following morning, the rain began the people were ready.

The rain came, and fell in torrents. There was no gradual buildup. The thick, black clouds had been so saturated that they were overzealous to relieve themselves of their burden, so for ten hours nonstop the rain poured.

Unlike most past hurricanes in which the wind snatched windows, doors and boards not securely attached, blew away roofs and strew galvanize and shingles all across the landscape, snapped coconut and mango trees like wire, and uprooted or bent sugarcane plants into uselessness, this hurricane wasn't accompanied by much wind. In fact, with so little wind, this October adventure hardly deserved the name hurricane. But it might have well been a hurricane. The rivers rose and swept across their flood plains, carrying and uprooting everything—sugarcane, bananas, cows, goats, sheep, houses, bridges—in their path. In the aftermath of nature's visitation, all except the people of L'Abbaye and Ravine Poisson offered their thanks to God that there was no loss of life.

To many of the people of L'Abbaye and Ravine Poisson, including Nelda and her family, there wasn't much for which to be thankful. Though they had been just as diligent as the rest of the island in preparing for the hurricane, God hadn't been as kind to them.

Among the people of L'Abbaye and Ravine Poisson, none had taken greater precaution than Nelda and her husband. With five kids ranging from age twelve to five-year-old Felina, they had taken no chances; they had stocked the house with an ample supply of rice, flour, yam, dasheen, tania, canned beef, saltfish, coffee, and coals. They had made sure there was enough kerosine to keep the three kerosine lamps in the house burning for days. Under the brooding clouds, Nelda's husband had climbed on top of the house, patched-up the roof and made sure each galvanized sheet was securely nailed down. And he had circled the house, nailing pieces of boards over holes and parts of the house that had begun to rot and needed reinforcement. He had made sure that the two doors in the house could be securely shut from the inside and he had barricaded the two windows on the windward side of the house by nailing boards across them. No one could have accused Nelda and her husband of negligence.

At two o'clock the morning following the day of the rains, the diligence of Nelda and her husband and the other people of L'Abbaye and Ravine Poisson came to nought. They had applied their diligence to what was above ground. But it was in the ground itself, the foundation upon which everything rested, that nature decided to focus its mischief. Their only salvation would have been to move their houses and themselves away from the Barré de l'Isle mountain range upon which sat L'Abbaye and Ravine Poisson.

All during the day the rain soaked the soil, which, at first, drank thirstily like a cow that had not drunk water in days, then, once quenched, grudgingly. The soil grew heavy, slippery, and as uncomfortable as a man who had drunk and eaten too much. To make way for homes and gardens, the people had cut down some of the trees that used to tie the soil unto its bedrock. So the restless soil was under less discipline than in the past and the road that had been cut in the mountainside to allow passage across the Barré de l'Isle now gave the soil space into which to move.

At two o'clock the morning following the day of the rains, Nelda awoke to a slight tremor, like that of a small earthquake, and immediately after, she heard a faint grumble that sounded like a cow mooing from afar. Then the grumble grew loud into the sound of trees crashing to the ground and the slight tremor became definite movement. The house began shaking as if a giant, holding the house at two of its corners, was shaking it free of its lumber-pillar foundations. She heard the sounds of pots and pans falling off the nails on which they hung and the sounds of chairs, the dining table, dressers, the book shelf, the sewing machine and everything that wasn't nailed down falling in disarray. Then she heard the frightening sound of the house cracking. Startled, she bolted up. Her husband had also got up.

"My God, the house is moving, the house is mashing up," said Nelda.

"Check on the girls," said her husband, "I'll check the boys."

Nelda hastened to her daughters' bedroom, calling out to them, calling out to God. But before she could get to her daughters, the house fell on its side and Nelda was flung against the side of the house. Her head hit wood and the lights went out.

When things had started falling, stricken with fright and half asleep, Felina had jumped into a large trunk half-filled with clothes and she had let the lid fall into place, burying herself from the chaos of the night. In the trunk she had heard her mother calling out to her and her sister; and she heard her sister screaming "Mama, Mama." She felt the house moving down, slowly at first, then more rapidly. The house fell on its side, and her newly found haven bumped and slid to the other end of the house. She fell unconscious with her mother's scream: "*Bondié, Bondié. Sé bout late, sé bout late,* God, God. The end of the world, the end of the world," ringing in her head.

The house slid down on its side on a river of mud, boulders, and plant debris, knocking into trees and other houses also on the move. Soon the house was no more a house, but a wreck and the wreck became splintered wood and debris, indistinguishable from the other debris the river of mud was carrying.

In the darkness of the night, the river of mud, boulders and debris carried or buried houses, trees, sheep, goats, cows, people, and everything else in its path, turning everything into a mass of debris. Soon the river of mud, boulders and debris crossed the road and piled up at the river flowing at the bottom of the valley.

The people of L'Abbaye and Ravine Poisson, those who lived on the outskirts of the night's river of disaster, those who had escaped the night's terror, woke up in the morning in shock. Never had they witnessed a calamity of such magnitude. Their twin village and its surroundings were transformed beyond recognition.

Except where the mud and debris had piled up, the land was as bare as when volcanic eruptions had just given birth to the island. It were as if someone with a giant scraper had savagely, but diligently, scraped the soil and everything rooted in it off the face of the land, leaving the bedrock naked and ugly.

Before the fortunate ones could drink their coffee, they fanned out in small groups searching over the desolation for brothers, sisters, mothers, fathers, grandparents, aunts, uncles; any survivor.

News of the disaster spread far and wide. Soon the search parties were joined by people from as far away as Castries and Dennery. They came not just to search for survivors and to offer material and emotional support, but to witness history.

History they did witness. They found arms cut off from bodies, lonely heads with mouth agape, crushed headless bodies, buried bodies with only arms showing, bodies with mouths filled with mud, whole families buried holding onto each other in a clutch of death.

Though few, they did find survivors. Some survivors had floated on the river of mud and had been deposited, beaten and unconscious, at the river flowing in the valley. Some were submerged in the mud and debris but hadn't suffocated because their heads were sticking out.

They found Felina unconscious in a partially submerged trunk, half-filled with clothes, resting against a lonely tree standing in the path of the landslide, not too far from the road. Nelda was also found alive. The search party who found her first saw movement in the mud twenty feet from where they were standing. Upon investigation they found a body thrashing weakly in the mud, or more accurately under the mud. She was faceup, and her partially surfaced head was indistinguishable from the surrounding mud and debris. If not for the movement in the mud, the search party could have passed a few feet away from her many times but never discover that this wasn't debris, but a human head. The rest of Nelda's family had perished.

The next day, when the search parties gave up hope of finding any more survivors, and the missing and the dead were counted, the people of the twin villages on the Barré de l'Isle found out they had ninety-two friends and relatives to mourn for, ninety-two friends and relatives for whom to hold an all night wake of coffee, rum, katumba, and stories of past disasters.

To find a catastrophe to match the havoc of the great landslide of 1938, the people had to go as far back as *en temp cholera* when the Asiatic Cholera claimed nearly fifteen hundred lives and sent the black population, just sixteen years removed from slavery, into such a marriage frenzy that the number of out of wedlock births went down by 25 percent. Yet whereas *en temp cholera* had taken the whole of three months to accomplish its work, the great landslide had needed only one night. The people of the twin villages had indeed witnessed history.

After witnessing the devastation brought upon his people, desolate in spirit, a Seventh Day Adventist preacher lost himself in a part of the forest untouched by the landslide, crying and begging God for forgiveness. At a Seventh Day Adventist tent crusade, several months before the landslide, in the throat of the dry season, with great passion and commiseration the preacher had warned the people of L'Abbaye and Ravine Poisson that the world was living on borrowed time, and if they didn't repent and turn away from their abominations—cockfights, fornication, adultery, bacchanal, whoremongering, defiling the temple of God with swine, rum, coffee, and all the other things that according to Deuteronomy, Chapter Eight, God had forbidden his people to eat—God would soon visit the land with plagues, pestilence, and disaster. The people of the twin villages had laughed at him, rebuked him, scorned him. They were a stubborn people. Some of the few the preacher was able to convert said to him: "*ou ka gaspiye tan-ou, jan L'Abbaye ek Ravine Poisson modi.*" "You are wasting your time, L'Abbaye and Ravine Poisson people are cursed."

Now God had heeded his cry and visited the people with a disaster of Biblical proportions. As the preacher walked aimlessly and unseeingly through the forest, apathetic to the many tree branches slapping his face, he cried to God: "Oh God. Oh God. Please, God, please, pardon me for my transgressions, my pride, my ego. I didn't mean what I said about visiting the people with pestilence and disaster. I didn't expect you to take my words spoken in frustration and self exultation so seriously. My life is worth nothing except to serve thee. Please God, take my life, but spare the rest of my people."

After this heart-to-heart talk with God, there was never before and never after a humbler preacher. After that day he spent less time trying to convert people and much more time caring for the needy. But in the few years following the great landslide of 1938, the Seventh Day Adventist preacher didn't need to threaten the people of the twin villages with fire and brimstone to get them to repent of their evil ways. What many preachers couldn't accomplish in twenty years, the landslide did in one night's work. In the weeks, months, and few years following the disaster, there wasn't enough room in the Adventist Church to hold the new converts. Never were the people of the twin villages so religious. The Adventist Church held baptisms in a stoneless part of the river flowing through the valley every two weeks for twelve months. For good measure, on top of the ten percent in tithes that the church said belonged to God, members donated another ten percent of their income in offerings. With the tithes and offerings and members' volunteered work, eighteen months after the great landslide, the Seventh Day Adventists of the twin villages completed one of the largest churches in the land. In an island almost 100 percent Roman Catholic, the Seventh Day Adventist Church had finally taken root. Even the now humbled preacher had to admit that God worked in mysterious ways.

The Seventh Day Adventist Church wasn't the only denomination to benefit from the disaster, nor were the people of

L'Abbaye and Ravine Poisson the only ones to rediscover their souls. All over the island the people took heed. At Roman Catholic Churches throughout the land, the line of people waiting to confess their iniquities stretched like marathons. For months to come, rumshops remained empty, cock fights ceased, husbands stayed home with their wives, and prostitutes went out of business.

Nelda slept through the rest of the day the search party found her, all of the night, and finally she woke up at one o'clock the next afternoon. Still in a state of delirium, she stared blankly around the room. It took her awhile to recognize Felina who, awakened an hour earlier, was anxiously waiting for her mother to wake up, not only to make sure that she was all right but to ask her about her father and siblings. Nelda had given Felina cause to worry. Asleep, Nelda had been clawing and pushing at the air like a crazy woman and she kept murmuring, "*Bondié, Bondié. Sé bout late, sé bout late.*" When Felina saw her mother's eyes open, she hurried and snuggled up to her, desperately seeking assurances that the happening of yesterday was just a momentary lapse, a dream, and today and the days to come would be like before. Much like the times her mother had spanked her for lying and after a few minutes of crying and what appeared to her as the end of the world, she had gone back to hanging onto her mother's dress, and getting in her way every where she went.

As her daughter sought her warmth, Nelda's eyes roved desperately around for her husband and her four other children. "Where your father and brothers and sisters?" She asked.

"I don't know, I thought you knew where they went."

Alarmed, Nelda looked around the room with greater focus and realized she was in a strange room, in a strange house.

Heartened by the voices emerging out of the room, Rosalyn, the woman of the house, Nelda's childhood friend, who upon finding out about the plight of her friend had insisted that the search party take her and the child to her house, hurried to see how her friend was doing. As she entered the bedroom, Nelda sat up from the bed and asked: "What happened? What I'm doing in your house? Where are my husband and children?"

Rosalyn looked at Nelda with great compassion. In spite of the thorough wash she had given Nelda before putting her to bed, brown grains of sand were still clinging to her hair. Normally calm and composed, Nelda had a haggard and wild look. The many hours of sleep didn't appear to have helped much. Rosalyn's eyes left Nelda's face and looked with pity on the tiny, confused child clinging desperately to her mother. Rosalyn hesitated to break the news.

"I thought you remembered," she said. "There was a massive landslide the night before that left nothing standing. Only by an act of God you and Felina were saved. They found you buried in dirt. Luckily you were still moving, or else they would have never found you. They found Felina in the large trunk your husband brought back from Cayenne. It was the trunk that saved her."

Nelda waited impatiently for her friend to mention her husband and the other children, but Rosalyn, not knowing how best to break the news, was hedging.

"What happened to my husband and children? Did they make it?" Nelda asked with rising apprehension.

Rosalyn approached the bed, sat on its edge, and stroked Nelda's head, plucking grains of sand from her hair, as if grooming her friend was the issue in question. Suppressing tears, she answered: "Nel, they didn't make it. The search parties couldn't find them, they didn't make it, they didn't make it."

With Felina crying and clinging to her, Nelda passed out, choosing oblivion over despair. Two hours later, she was rolling, rolling, rolling in a mountain of soil and her body came to a stop against a log and the mountain of soil started piling on top of her, choking her. Desperately, she clawed, and clawed at the soil, trying to make her way out of the dirt. But the more she clawed and pushed, the more dirt that piled on top of her. Soon she couldn't breathe and then everything went black. In her delirium, the dream repeated itself again and again, until finally she clawed her way out of the mountain of dirt and opened her eyes to find Felina shaking her and sobbing, "Mama, wake up! Wake up! Don't die! Don't die!"

Nelda sat up suddenly as the fate of her husband and children penetrated her consciousness. Her only thoughts were: Oh God, I got to find them, I got to find them. Forgetting she wasn't at her home, she got out of bed and began searching for her clothes to change out of the nightie Rosalyn had dressed her in twenty-seven hours earlier.

Hearing the commotion, Rosalyn hurried to the room. She found Nelda rummaging through the worn out mahogany chest in the room. "What you looking for?" asked Rosalyn.

Not looking up, Nelda answered, "I got to find them, Rosalyn, I got to find them."

"Here, let me help."

Rosalyn gave her friend one of her everyday-wear dresses.

She said, "you and your daughter haven't eaten anything for over twenty-four hours, before you go at least have some soup." But what she gave Nelda and Felina couldn't be called soup. It was a broth of fish, pumpkin, yam, and green figs— a meal in and of itself. Both mother and daughter devoured the food. The daughter out of hunger, the mother out of haste to go and search for her husband and children.

After they had eaten, Rosalyn again tried to delay her friend. "Nel, the search parties have searched everywhere, some are still searching. If your husband and children can be found, they will find them. It is already afternoon, soon the sun will be going down. Stay and rest, there will be plenty of time tomorrow to look."

Waving her hands in disagreement, Nelda, with Felina holding on to her dress, headed for the door. Rosalyn had no choice but to accompany her friend.

Now that the sky had relieved itself of its burden, it had

regained its usual blue. The sun had no problems penetrating the calm, white clouds, so although it was late afternoon the land was well lighted. Disturbed by the rains, flying insects filled the air, getting into eyes and sores. Unsympathetic to the human disaster, everywhere the landslide had left untouched, grass and shrubs were rioting in their new found glory brought about by the rains.

Arriving at the site of nature's wrath, flanked by her child-hood friend and her only surviving child, Nelda looked into the distance to where her house and surrounding farm should be. But in place of her homestead a desolate and gorged landscape greeted her. The land from which she had reaped an abundance of fruits, vegetables and ground provisions was now reduced to clay-red bedrock. She knew then that she had not only lost her family but her homestead also. She suddenly became weak and her knees buckled. Rosalyn quickly wrapped her arms around her friend and sat her on a log as gently as she would a sleeping child.

3

About 1:00 P.M., Friday, June 13, 1893, the gods of the land cast their eyes over Castries, their nemesis, and noticed a ship approaching harbor. Upon closer examination the gods counted six hundred and forty-three Indians in the belly of the ship. The gods were perplexed. "Didn't we destroy all of these Carib savages? Then what are they doing in our waters?" The gods looked at the bold white letters, *VOLGA*, written on the sides of the ship, but the name meant nothing to them. Then the gods were forced to admit that a few of the savages had slipped their grip the first time around. "This time there will be no such blunder," they said. And they decided to bury all six hundred and forty-three of what they thought were Caribs at the bottom of the Caribbean Sea. So the gods sent a sudden gust that ripped apart the ship's sails and whipped the sea into six-foot waves. The ship began tossing recklessly, the sea started filling the ship and the Indians in the ship's belly started screaming and praying to their Hindu gods in their Hindu dialects. It was their prayers that saved them, not because their Hindu gods had answered their prayers, as the Indians would later recount and celebrate, but because when the gods of the land heard their language they realized that it wasn't the language of

38

the Caribs. This was a language that had been refined by writing, so they had not made a blunder, after all. The gods then reined in the wind, the sea became calm, the ship settled, and, skirting the rocks, eased gently toward Vigie Point. Soon, fishing canoes, two steamships at anchor, and everything in the Castries and Gros Islet area that could float came to the rescue. All six hundred and forty-three of the Caribs turned Indians on board the immigrant ship, *VOLGA*, were rescued. For years to come the rescued Indians would continue to offer special thanks and sacrifices to their Hindu gods for saving their lives on the day of the Shipwrecked Indians. So much so that the gods of the land came to regret ever saving their lives.

Among the six hundred and forty-three Indians was Valda Girade, the grandmother of Christine. But unlike most of her fellow Indian immigrants, she hadn't given thanks to her Hindu gods for saving her life. On the contrary, after the humiliation and despair of being tricked and sold, of never seeing her parents again in this life; after three months traversing two oceans, moving down the waters of the Indian subcontinent to the frigid waters of the Cape of Good Hope and back up to the tropical waters of the South Atlantic and the Caribbean sea; after three months of doom, emptiness and seasickness, of dark, damp, overcrowded, rat-infested, tomb-like quarters, she just couldn't care whether she was dead or alive. Long before the *VOLGA* had entered the Caribbean Sea, she had wished she were one of those who had died of unnamed sickness and been thrown overboard, one of those who had been given a sea burial.

Valda's voyage to the land of the twin peaks, the land of the gods, began on March 18, 1880, at the age of five, when she was promised to a boy of another village forty miles away. Two days past her thirteenth birthday, a year after she first saw her womanhood, she wedded. And oh, how colorful, how beautiful, how exciting, how exhilarating the wedding had been!

The wedding began in midafternoon. Valda was dressed in

a splendid, multicolored saree, a red blouse, and her head was covered with golden ornaments. Her neck decked with gold necklaces, and her gold nose ring shone like the sun. In all she wore thirty talas of gold, the amount agreed upon as part of the dowry from her family to the groom's family. The bride and groom sat on a small wooden platform in the marriage hall. Crowding the marriage hall were the groom's family and the bride's entire village. Directly in front of the bride and groom was the wedding priest standing next to a bonfire set in a rectangular wall. The priest chanted, prayed, and called on the god of fire, the god of water, and the god of fertility. Ever so often, in the mid of his chanting, the priest sprinkled, sometimes milk, sometimes ghee, into the fire—offerings to the gods.

A few times, while the priest was summoning up the gods, Valda stole glances at her husband to be. The white cloth wrapped around his lower body contrasted sharply with his bare upper body. Gold strands hung from his white turban. He looks so strong, she thought, so much like a warrior king. I'm going to bear him many sons. He will not regret having me for a wife.

The groom didn't steal glances at his wife soon to be. The veil she was wearing made this pointless. Not until the bridal bed would he see her face.

The priest had summoned the gods. The gods had given their blessings. The priest's duty was complete. He beckoned to the bride and groom. As in a trance, the bride and groom circled the fire. Seven times. And they were wed. The priest and guests threw rice on the husband and wife—be fruitful and multiply. Under the rice shower, Valda hoped and prayed that all her fruits would be boys. She would not disappoint her husband; she would not disappoint her family. Her family would soon find out that their dowry was wealth well spent.

The wedding feast began in the early evening, and carried on all night. Never before had Valda seen so much food. On green banana leaves lay all types of rice specialities, all types of curried vegetable dishes, all types of kheers. And throughout the feast, throughout the night, the band played classical Eastern music. Oh how sweet, how romantic, how soothing was the music! The flute, the tabla, the sitar, the violin and the shehnai fusing into one sound, as if all the sounds were coming from one and the same instrument. Valda barely touched the food. She was filled with its aroma, the music that soothed, tantalized and transported her to distant worlds, and the colorful sarees, the turbans, the silver and gold ornaments adorning the women.

The next day came, and it was time to depart. Time to begin the forty mile journey to her husband's village. For the first time in her life Valda was stepping out of her village. She had never ventured beyond the rice fields. It was a tearful goodbye. Valda clung to her mother, refusing to let go. "I am not going," she said. "I am not going. Please mama, don't let them take me."

Her mother, also in tears, held her and waited for her sobbing to subside. It was always the same. The mother, herself, had sobbed just as much when it was her turn fifteen years ago to leave her family and join her husband in a strange village. So did her mother before her. The daughter could sob, she could fill the Ganges with tears, but nothing would change. In the same way it hadn't changed for the mother now holding her sobbing daughter in her arms or for the grand mother before the mother.

Valda's fate was sealed eight years ago when a marriage broker brought to the attention of her parents a boy of another village, and acted as the go-between, finalizing the transaction, and negotiating the dowry Valda's family would have to pay the boy's family.

Valda's grasp finally weakened, and the mother, holding her daughter around the shoulders, the daughter's head cradled on the mother's breasts, walked her daughter to the ox-drawn cart that would take the daughter, the husband and the husband's family all of the eight miles to the train station. They would take the train to within three miles of the husband's village and then they would ride to the village on another ox-drawn cart.

Trouble began within hours of Valda's arrival at her new home. Her mother-in-law complained that the gold which Valda wore at the wedding was short of what was agreed upon as part of the dowry. And on top of that, the rice, the other part of the dowry, was filthy and had begun to rot. This clouded the mother-in-law's vision. The girl whom she saw at the wedding as radiantly beautiful and who had been the envy of everyone in attendance had suddenly become scrawny and sickly and unfit for her son. Soon, in the eyes of the mother-in-law, Valda could do no right. And since the husband took his cues from his mother, in his eyes, also, Valda was less than adequate. He beat his wife often and most times for imagined wrongs. Valda's predicament grew worse when, after two years of consummated marriage, she was yet to produce her husband a son, or any child for that matter. The beatings and the nagging increased in frequency and intensity. By then if Valda could, she would have gladly run back home. But she didn't know her way back, nor was it clear that if she had made her way back, her parents would have accepted her. The disgrace to the family might have been too much to bear.

So after three childless years, both mother-in-law and daughter-in-law, though for different reasons, were looking for a way out of this arrangement. And it was around this time that an indentured servant hunter in search of recuits to work the sugar plantations of the British West Indies made his presence known. The sugar plantations were desperate for cheap labor because recently released from several hundred years of slavery, the ex-slaves weren't too excited about working the white man's sugar plantations, as if they were still in bondage. Not when they could cultivate their ground provisions and other produce on the hills and mountains, lands unfit for sugar cultivation, lands the plantation owners called marginal lands. It was one thing to say slavery was abolished, but another to break the centuries old habits of dependency and subjugation. The subsistence these mountains, these marginal lands, afforded the ex-slaves went as far in unclasping their shackles as the proclamation of emancipation.

So soon after slavery, the plantations, unwilling to pay more than token wages to people they once had for free, quickly ran into a labor shortage. Their unwillingness to pay higher wages was not just a matter of taste, however; it was a matter of survival. They were now competing with slave-grown sugar from Brazil and Cuba. The Spanish and Portuguese nobles, unlike those of England who were among the first to relieve their citizens of the burden of the slave trade and slavery, had not yet seen fit to extend their nobility to the slaves of their empire. Partly a response to the labor shortage and partly to offset the overwhelmingly black population of the islands, the plantation owners attempted to recruit white workers. But disease, death, and an unwillingness to do work once set aside for slaves, niggers, made many of the few white recruits the plantations were able to obtain of little use. Spoiled by years of slave labor, free labor, black labor, the plantations then went to Africa for recruits. But the Africans, having barely missed the slave ships, were no more excited to cross the Atlantic Ocean on promises of a better life than were their shackled predecessors. So the African immigrants were even fewer than the white recruits. This left the Indian subcontinent, colonized by the same masters of the owners of the sugar plantations of the British West Indies, as the de facto source of cheap labor.

By 1893, fifty-six years after the first Indian indentured servants arrived on the shores of the British West Indies, most of the Indians in the city ports of Madras, Calcutta, and Bombay, who were willing and able to migrate to the Caribbean as indentured servants had already done so. The news of the many deaths suffered on the journey, and the slave-like work and living conditions of the plantations that had filtered back to the cities and villages of India did not help the recruiting effort. So, not unlike bounty hunters, indentured-servant hunters were now forced to venture into the countryside for recruits, and, with a bounty on every person they recruited, they weren't too particular about how they got their recruits. And since the bounty on women was now almost as high as that on men, women would do just as well as men.

The plantations had increased the reward for women indentured servants because there was a paucity of Indian women to wed the abundance of Indian men on the plantations and the plantations had begun to realize that a man with a wife and children was less bold, less likely to cause trouble, less willing to revolt against the slave-like life he was forced to live and jeopardize the one shilling a day he was receiving for his slave-like labor. And with the going daily wage for women being eight pence and for children, four pence, the plantation owners quickly learned that a plantation of family labor, not unlike what existed in slavery, made more economic sense than a plantation of solitary men. Furthermore, a man with his family was less willing to brave the oceans and return home after his five-years of servitude were over, thus ensuring the plantation of continued cheap labor. Not that the plantations often kept their promise of a return passage home after the indentured servants had completed their bondage.

So with an indentured-servant hunter heedless of the gender of his recruits and how they obtained them—by trickery, or by outright kidnapping—a daughter-in-law who was desperate to abandon her husband and return to her parents, a husband who thought of his wife as a disservice, a disgrace, and a mother-in-law looking for ways to get rid of her daughter-in-law, Valda's fate was sealed. The indentured-servant hunters presented the husband and mother-in-law with a more palatable and profitable way of getting rid of Valda than burning her alive as some less fortunate wives and daughters-in-laws could speak of from the grave.

The mother-in-law asked her neighbor to gain Valda's confidence and to express to Valda a willingness to direct her to her village. On the appointed day of the journey to Valda's village, both her husband and her mother-in-law were conspicuously absent:

her husband was out working in his rice paddies, her mother-in-law out visiting a sister who lived a mile away. Valda and her neighbor walked to the train station and took the train, supposedly bound for Valda's village. After several stops and several hours on the train, Valda had become alarmed. It didn't seem that on her previous trip the train had taken as much time and had made as many stops. But the neighbor told her that this was a different train. This train had a more roundabout route. Finally, after ten hours on the train, the neighbor told her that this was their stop. Valda got off the train and though it was night, she had no trouble realizing that this city was much bigger than the town from which she had caught the train that had brought her to her husband's village. By then Valda was deeply troubled and perplexed. Something was terribly wrong. They had probably taken the wrong train. Again the neighbor soothed her fears. "No, this isn't the town close to your village. I told you we took a roundabout route. We are in Calcutta. We will have to spend a few days here and wait for the boat that will take you to another city and from there you will take a train to the town close to your village. Things have changed. There is no more a direct train to the town close to your village."

Valda was illiterate. In her thirteen years of living in her village, she had never gone further than her parents rice paddies and the homes of her relatives. In her husband's village she had been even more confined. Names like Calcutta, Bombay and Madras were as foreign to her as London, New York, and Paris. She had no choice but to trust her neighbor.

In Calcutta Valda and her neighbor slept in a barrack-like building close to the port. The building was crowded with people waiting for the boat. On Valda's second day of waiting a doctor accompanied by another man medically examined her and told his companion that she was fit and healthy for the journey. Then following instructions, she placed an X several places on sheets of paper with writings on them. Then she saw the man accompanying the doctor give her neighbor some money, and wondered why the man was giving her money for the boat trip, when it should be the other way around. Valda was still ignorant of her fate.

On the morning of her fifth day she and the other people at the barracks began boarding the *VOLGA*. Not waiting for the ship to leave, her neighbor waved her goodbye and walked briskly toward the train station. An hour later, the ship blew its departure horn and slowly moved away from port. Then, suddenly, a shriek and frantic wave distracted the sadness of both the people on the ship and on land who were still waving each other goodbye.

"Valda, it's a trick, a trick. They are taking you away. Oh God, oh God, they have stolen my baby. Valda, make them turn the ship back. It's a trick, a trick. Come back. Come back."

It was Valda's mother. The woman who had taken Valda to Calcutta had, against her sworn promise to the mother-in-law, confided in a neighbor that the mother-in-law was shipping Valda away to the West Indies. The neighbor, against her sworn promise to her neighbor, had wasted no time in sending word to Valda's mother. But the mother was a few minutes too late. Her daughter's fate was sealed.

In an instant, upon hearing the words "trick, trick, come back, come back," everything became clear to Valda: the ten-hour train ride, the wait in the barracks, the medical examination, the exchange of money, even the *X* marks. She had been sold. She had heard stories of parents selling their children or husbands selling their wives, but she had treated such stories as things that happened in strange, faraway places, not in her village or a village only forty miles away. In the instant of her mother's screams, she comprehended her predicament. Valda's screams drowned those of her mother. And she ran to the side of the boat to fling herself into the water. But the sailors were prepared. They had seen it all before. Every time a ship was sailing off with Indian immigrants there was always one or two who, suddenly realizing that they might never see their family and friends again, never again lay eyes on their village, their country, would become frantic, and if not held down, would jump ship. One of the sailors grabbed Valda, and ignoring her scratches, her writhing body, half dragged, half carried her to a cabin. And as he was turning the keys, locking the cabin, sealing Valda's fate, he was thinking: she is so thin and frail, looking at her, who would have thought she had that much fight in her; exactly the kind of fight she will need to survive the three months at sea.

4

Seven-year-old Felina, dressed in a starched-white bodice tucked into a sky-blue skirt reaching to her knees, was standing on the wharf under the shade of the custom duties building, waiting to catch the attention of her mother, Nelda, who was occupied with a life and death coal-loading odyssey. Felina unconsciously touched her hair, which was plaited into small black screws. Beads of sweat on her coal-black forehead spoke of her walk in the two o'clock heat from the Girls' School.

Not for the first time, Felina looked in awe at the mountains of coals that seemed to dwarf not only the pier and the three coal-steam ships anchored at port but also the collection of white-walled, red-roofed, two-story buildings that made up most of the city, stretched across the waterfront, and climbed to the hills that imprisoned the city from the back. To Felina, it was not the Caribbean Sea that imprisoned the city from the front, but the mountains of coal.

Felina was not alone in her impression. A year later, on December 18, 1940, she and her school mates would have the pleasure of waving to President Franklin D. Roosevelt as he toured the Castries Harbor on the U.S. Cruiser Tuscaloosa, escorted by two destroyers. A collection of white, red-roofed buildings imprisoned from the back by mountains of green and from the front by mountains of black was the image of Castries that stayed with the President long after his tour of the harbor was completed.

Felina looked at her bare feet and though she knew her efforts were futile, she rubbed them against the building, trying to dislodge the coal-dust clinging to them. Her feet weren't the only things to which coal dust was clinging. If she were to look back the way she came, she would see her tiny foot prints in the layer of coal dust that covered the waterfront and everything standing near it. And if she were to stand long enough at the pier, she would have difficulty deciphering the original color of her now starched-white bodice, just like it was now impossible for a visitor to decipher that the two-story buildings close to the pier that the coal-dust had turned to yellowish-brown were once chalk-white.

Felina's attention shifted from her coal-stained feet to her mother and the other coal-stained charbonniers loading one of the ships with coal. The women's heads were wrapped with madras, and their waists were tightly wound with cloths of the same color as the madras. Pads resembling miniature pillows were anchored on their heads by a string tied under their chin.

Felina's eyes followed the women as they left the ship with their empty dome-shaped, bamboo-thatched baskets. Upon leaving the ship, each woman collected a copper token from a crippled man seated on the pier at the foot of the ramp linking the ship to the pier. The man's sole function was to dispense tokens to the women for each basket of coal they deposited in the ship's bosom and to tally the number of such baskets.

The women dug between their breasts, brought up coal-stained cloths, unknotted the cloths, added the newly earned tokens to their collection, retied the cloths and slipped them back between their breasts. With their newly earned tokens secured, they brushed off the coal dust from their clothes and moved on toward one of the mountains of coals.

They laid their baskets at the foot of the mountain, and, using shovels, barebacked men covered with coal dust and sweat filled the baskets with coal, and with the women holding on to one end of the baskets and the men the other, the hundredweight baskets of coal were loaded onto the women's heads. Then, with backs straight as electric posts, necks taut as pulleys, faces determined and shining with sweat and coal dust, the women gracefully hurried toward the ship like goddesses carrying oversized umbrellas. They climbed the ramp, entered the ship, descended to the ship's coal-storage room and deposited their loads, coal dust rising to their faces.

One of the other ships anchored at port was a coal-carrier. Tomorrow the charbonniers would have the pleasure of unloading the coal ship in the same manner they were now refueling the ship that Felina was watching them move in and out of. But instead of unmaking the mountain of coals, they would be rebuilding it. And when, like a pyramid, the mountain rose above their reach, they would climb a steep ramp to dump their hundredweight cargos on top of the heap, as if to outdo the pyramids their distant ancestors decreed.

Felina was both awed and saddened by the sight of her mother straining under the hundredweight baskets of coal. She was thinking, wasn't there a better way, an easier way? At the end of the day one shilling was the most her mother would have to show for eight hours of breathing in coal dust and working like a mule in the tropical sun. A measly shilling that could buy at most one and one-half pounds of fresh beef, or two and one-half pounds of fresh fish, or five pounds of rice or flour. God is to blame, Felina was thinking. God is to blame.

Felina still couldn't find it in her heart to forgive God for snatching away her father and two brothers and two sisters. Over and over, at Sunday Mass, in her catechism class, at school, she heard of the grace, mercy and goodness of God. But she couldn't help but ask, "if God is so kind and merciful, how could he allow

50

the landslide to make her father and siblings disappear from the face of the earth, though not from her dreams and memory; the same God Who was now subjecting her mother to this donkey work, this slave-labor?"

To Felina, there was no more godly, no more pious, no more kind, no more giving a person than her mother. In her mind, if there was one person on earth that God should be merciful to, it would have to be her mother. But as she watched her mother under the one hundredweight basket of coal, and when she saw her in the late afternoon covered with coal-dust, dragging her weary soul back home, Felina knew there was no mercy in that.

Felina learned to kneel, fold her hands, murmur her *Hail Marys* and picture angels in their winged glories hovering over her, protecting her from evil. She learned to recite the Lord's Prayer and envision a Christ so merciful in His whiteness that He gave His life on Calvary's Cross so she, little Felina, could go to heaven. Every Sunday she accompanied her mother to Sunday Mass and was awed by the many statues—the crucifixion, Saint Peter, Saint Paul, Christ in a stable surrounded by Mary, Joseph, and wise men from the East. Yet Felina still cherished a grain of doubt about God's mercy, because where it mattered most to her, God didn't seem to care, or for that matter, God had gone out of His way to be the opposite of merciful.

As Felina matured the grain of doubt would swell. So that at the age of twelve, when Nelda stopped monitoring Felina's nightly prayer ritual, Felina would abandon prayer. It was hard at first. Felina was fighting against twelve years of conditioning. Every night when she lay down in bed, a small voice kept reminding her that she had not prayed. The voice kept saying, "go kneel and pray; you haven't asked God forgiveness for the day's wrongs; you haven't given him thanks for keeping you and your mother alive and for putting food on the table."

Felina stopped praying not because she stopped believing there was a God, but because she stopped believing in the goodness and mercy of God. Her refusal to pray was her way of punishing God for his atrocities against her murdered father and siblings and the hardship she and her mother were undergoing. As time went on the disturbing voice that had kept her awake far into the night grew fainter and fainter, until finally, it was as if she had never known prayer. She was glad to be rid of the voice altogether, but her priest would have told her that the spirit of God had left her, probably for good.

Eight months after Felina stopped praying, she would pray one more time, and that would be the last time she would ever lend her breath to prayer. It was the night of the barking dogs. At two o'clock on a Sunday night Felina was awakened by a barrage of dog barks. Nights were usually punctuated with occasional dog barks, but this Sunday night was different. For no explainable reason the neighborhood dogs had gone crazy. In the midst of the continuous barking, Felina heard persistent racking-coughs. Her mother often coughed during the night but they were usually isolated coughs followed by long periods of silence or snores. Tonight her mother's coughs were matching the barks of the dogs in intensity and stubbornness. Worried, Felina parted the cloth curtain that divided the one bedroom in the shack into her and her mother's sleeping quarters. In the dim moonlight piercing through the opened wooden louvers, Felina found her mother in a pool of blood, murmuring something indecipherable.

She immediately fell down on her knees, on the bed, gripped her mother by the shoulders and begged, "please, mama, please, don't die, don't die." And on her knees, on the bed, Felina prayed for the first time in eight months.

"Please God. Please, please, please. Don't let my mother die. You have taken my father, my two sisters and my two brothers, so please God don't take my mother too. Forgive me for having stopped praying, for not giving thanks to you over the past eight months. If you save my mother, I promise that I will give my life wholeheartedly to you, I will serve you all the days of my life, even more than my mother served you. If you want, I will even become a nun."

While Felina prayed the dogs' barks grew louder, and her mother's coughs grew weaker and weaker. And at two-thirty that night Nelda breathed her last breath, Felina prayed her last prayer, and never again was Felina to set foot in a church.

Watching the charbonniers, Felina knew as sure as the coal was black that God was to blame for her and her mother's misfortunes. Wasn't it her very aunt, her mother's sister, who upon arriving at L'Abbaye from Castries a few days after the landslides to check on the welfare of her sister, had immediately proclaimed the havoc of the landslides God's curse on the twin villages, and then implored her sister to leave this God forsaken place and come with her to Castries where her sister was sure to find work?

Nelda's sister wasn't aware of the different type of curse, but nonetheless just as destructive, that the gods had placed on Castries. She hadn't mentioned that eleven years ago the fire of the gods had destroyed seventeen blocks of the city she was dangling in front of her sister. And she couldn't have known the extent of the gods' anger against Castries and that the gods would visit Castries again and again. Neither could she have known that the calamity on the Barre de l'Isle was a mistake. The gods had mistaken the Barre de l'Isle for Morne Fortune and the other hills surrounding Castries. It was the gods' intention for the avalanche to start at the top of the hills surrounding Castries and to bury the city from the foot of the hills to the Caribbean Sea. After that mistake, the gods pledged to stick to their original design for the city—fire.

For her part, Nelda had not needed much encouragement from her sister or any one else to leave the land that held only sorrow for her, the land that had murdered her husband and children and had turned her homestead into uselessness. With no land to cultivate, no husband to bring home a miserly one shilling and four pence after a day in the hot, muddy, mosquito and rat infested cane-fields, she was more than willing to follow her sister to the city.

In every one of the years between 1926 and 1939, not only Felina, but the whole island had reason to believe that God had forsaken their land. The sugar industry, the heart and soul of the country, the reason for enslaving a race and for forcing, tricking, kidnaping Indians from India into servitude, was into irreversible decline. And in 1927, in addition to the fire of the gods which had turned the heart of the capital city into ashes and rubble, Panama Disease had wiped out the fledgling banana industry, and wither-tip and blossomblight had devastated the lime industry.

Unknown to Felina, Nelda had to consider herself lucky for the donkey work, because by the time they had arrived in Castries, the city's role as a coal fueling station was long in decline as other forms of fuel were replacing coal. And on top of everything else came the island-wide landslides, and the floods of 1938—the cause of the child's grief and hatred of God—that shattered the island's infrastructure and over half of its agriculture.

The construction of a U.S. naval base in the Castries area and an army base in the southern fishing town of Vieux Fort, and other U.S. World War II military activities, would soon give the island an economic boost. And when the last of the Americans would pack up and leave, the banana industry would finally take root and set in motion a social, political and economic transfor-mation. But even so, the years of 1927 through 1939, the years that historians would later label the years of "effort and trial" would linger long in the island's memory.

But unlike Felina, Nelda didn't blame God for her predica-ment. On the contrary, she was thankful to God for sparing her daughter's life. She didn't try to understand why it was she and her daughter God had saved and not the rest of her family. It had never occurred to her to question the work of God; she didn't think she was qualified. Nelda remained devoted to God and stead-fast in her Roman Catholic faith. Until her death she never missed a Sunday mass, and as long as she could help it her daughter didn't either. There never was a more dependable member of the church; the priest could always count on her to bake and cook for church bazaars, to weed around the church and to help sweep and tidy the church for mass. With her rosaries for comfort and fortitude, she repeated her Hail Mary's and the Lord's Prayer first thing in the morning and last thing before her weary head hit the night's pillow.

She never touched liquor. Never. Not even after or during a day's coal-carrying odyssey did she wash the coal dust from her throat with a shot of white rum or whiskey, like her fellow charbonniers were in the habit of doing. She never visited a dance hall, or touched a cigarette, or smoked a pipe. Her only vice, if you could call it that, was that she had a sweet tooth. A candy every now and then was one of the few pleasures she allowed herself. The other pleasure was caring for her sole remaining child and watching her blossom.

Though she was only thirty-eight when her husband died, she never looked at another man. It was as if she had divorced her husband and married the church. The love and devotion she once lavished on her husband, she now gave to the church. No, unlike the daughter, the mother never did abandon God.

Not when the land that had once sustained her family wiped out her husband and children in one night's work; not when, after a day's work, she returned to her shack with aching bones, tired muscles and a stiff neck; not when after several years of breathing in coal dust she started suffering from silicosis and acquired a persistent cough and occasionally spat blood. Not even when, seven years after she left the land that had murdered her family and turned her homestead into uselessness, in the same hour that the landslide had buried her family, during the night of the barking dogs, an uncontrollable cough had taken over her body and she began to cough-up a continuous stream of blood and she knew that she would not see the morning in spite of her daughter who was holding her shoulders as tight as the grip of death, as if that would stop her body from convulsing with each cough, and who was begging her not to die, and was praying to God, for the first time in a long time, to save her mother and in return she would serve God with all her heart, even onto death.

No. Instead of cursing God, as her daughter had done after the landslide and again after God had not answered her prayers and allowed her mother to join her father and brothers and sisters in death, Nelda had used her last breath to thank God for saving the life of her daughter seven years ago, and to ask God to watch over her daughter and let the world be more kind to her daughter and her daughter's children than it had been to her and her family.

On Nelda's death bed, the gods of the land had heard her prayer, and if Nelda wasn't so near to death, she might have heard or sensed the derision of the gods of her death plea. If she had gotten such an inkling, she would not have died with as much certainty as she did about the well-being of her daughter and her daughter's children.

The neighborhood dogs had felt the suffering of the dying woman and they had sensed the plan the gods had for the woman's daughter and the first grandchild of the woman, so they wailed throughout the night. So what the daughter thought were barks on the night of the barking dogs, were not barks at all, but wails of despair.

Felina's wondering gaze shifted from the charbonniers and steam ships to the calm waters of the Caribbean. Straight ahead she could see Vigie and Latoc Points, which partially enclosed the harbor. The protection these two points afforded the harbor and Castries was what was responsible for making Castries and therefore St. Lucia such a historically coveted estate, and for the French moving the capital from Soufrière to Castries at the displeasure of the gods of the land.

Felina looked beyond the points into the open sea. As often happened, when she gazed over the vastness of the Caribbean Sea, she began to reflect in a dreamlike state about her past and her future. Felina thought about her father and brothers and sisters. They were never far away from her mind. At nights she dreamed of them often, and sometimes woke up in tears, crying for her father and calling out to her brothers and sisters. Felina was never quite clear about the details of the landslide, how she and her mother survived.

Her mother refused to talk about it. After her mother had recovered from two months of grief and of wanting oblivion, she locked the landslide in a mental compartment, to think about it from time to time, and went about the business of living and caring for her daughter.

Though Felina was never clear about what had happened during the fateful night of the landslide, she had a recurring dream that began that night, so she sensed that the dream had something to do with the landslide. There were many variations to the dream—she fell into a pit toilet, she was swallowed by a boa-constrictor, she was drowning in the dark depths of the Caribbean Sea—but always, she was choking, choking, and it was dark, dark, darker than night. Always, she would wake up screaming.

In the early morning or late afternoon she would sometimes relate her dream to Nelda, but Nelda, knowing the source of the dream and not wanting to bring back the pain was always non-committal.

With such a painful past and a sorrowful and austere present, the seven-year-old child gazing over the waters of the Caribbean, waiting for her mother to take a respite from her neck-breaking labor, day dreamed of a sunshine future, a future that didn't include manual labor and slaving under hundredweight baskets of coal or any other load, for that matter. Slavery was long gone, Felina reckoned. In that sunshine future, she fell in love with the most handsome man in the land. A man not necessarily rich, but with ambition as wide as the ocean. Hand in hand, they worked their way to riches; by way of business—a grocery store, a restaurant, a clothes store—the particulars varied. They built their house where no landslide, or flooding river, or roaring sea could venture. They grew old together, nurtured and watched their nine children come of age, marry and bear children of their own. This was the dream that the child of the twin villages, the child of the landslides, daydreamed every time she came to meet her mother at the black mountains which together with the charbonniers conjured up the cruelties of the past, and the Caribbean Sea the possibilities of the future.

5

They met as planned. At four o'clock Sunday afternoon when the sun was well on its way down. It was the perfect day, the perfect time. On Sunday the Indian village of Forestierè rested from the cane fields, the vegetable gardens, and the ground provision plots. And by 4 P.M. Forestierè had already given unto God the part of the day that belonged to Him. The men were gathered around Forestierè's rumshop alongside the road and were long into their cockfights, dominoes, rum, and country and western music. The women had already plaited each other's hair, had oiled their skins with coconut oil, and were playing spectators to the men who were getting rowdier by the minute.

Occupied with getting drunk and affirming their manhood, Julita's father and six brothers had no time for worrying about her bringing shame to the family and to their manhood. Valda and the other women of Forestiere were either too busy satisfying their men's craving for attention or making sure their men didn't drink all of the meager week's pay (that sweating in the cane fields and cocoa orchards six days a week, ten hours a day, had brought their family) to notice the whereabouts of Julita and the other girls of the village who they assumed were grouped somewhere, carrying on silly.

It was the perfect place; past the cane fields, past the dasheen lagoon, past the yam patches, past the mango trees pregnant with fruit, and into the largely untouched forest a few feet from the creek. On Sunday afternoons no man, woman or child, except those who wanted and needed secrecy or solitude, would be found that deep into the woods. They met in the woods under a white cedar tree next to a cashew nut tree pregnant with yellow cashew fruit. They needed all the secrecy, if not the solitude, they could get. Julita was already promised to another, another of her race. By agreeing to meet Leonce, a boy of the other race, the black race, she was violating three thousand years of tradition. They met nervously, they smiled shyly, not speaking, just smiling. There was no need for words. They held hands self consciously, as if unsure of the purpose of their meeting. This was the first time they had dared to go so far. A fleeting look, a wink, a smile, a few words in passing were all they had managed.

Since Leonce had first seen Julita at a bursar at Forestierè, he had walked the four miles between Babonneau and Forestierè many times, and most times his only reward was a smile, a passing word, a coy look that said, "I like you too." For a year that had been enough to keep him walking, but finally he had to have more. He became bold, and with Julita's brothers looking on he told her they would have to meet because he was no longer willing to walk all that way just for a look at her. It had been painful for Julita too and it had hurt her to see Leonce walking all that way for nothing. She could not lose him, so she agreed to meet him this Sunday.

He should take the path, past the cane fields, past the dasheen lagoon, past the yam patches, past the mango julee trees pregnant with ripening fruit and enter the woods and keep on walking until he could hear the stream. She would meet him there at four when the sun was on its way down, two hours before dusk. There they would have all of two hours to themselves.

When Leonce was leaving one of Julita's brothers shouted,

"hey neg, noir kon charbon, pa vini isi-a ankò. Hey nigger, black as charcoal, don't come here again." Leonce ignored the brothers. His mission was accomplished. The brothers then turned to their sister, scolding her. "Ain't she ashamed of carrying on like a *salòp,* a *jamet,* slut, speaking to that neg, that slave, black as coals?" The older brother slapped her, leaving the print of his hands on her face, and told her to never let him see her talking to this neg or any neg again. She looked down and bore the pain in silence. Sunday, among the woods, two hours from dusk, awaited.

Coal-black hands held copper-brown hands, nervously, tentatively, tenderly. Coal-black hands slid ever so softly over copper-brown arms, disturbing the hairs coating the copper-brown skin. Thick, dark lips brushed against thin, pink lips; straight, black hair mingled with, covered, black, woollen hair. Heart beats quickened, the lovers grew weak. They lay down under the white cedar tree next to the fruit-laden cashew nut tree on a carpet of dry leaves. The dry leaves crunched under the lovers' embrace, and the nearby stream sang sweet melodies. Coal-black skin covered copper-brown skin. Africa joined India in a crucible of love. Enthralled by the sharing of a forbidden fruit, the young lovers did not hear the fall of a cashew nut too ripe to remain hanging, nor the begging sounds of a pair of blackbird chicks, as the parents fed them supper in a nest high up in the white cedar tree. Spent, the lovers remained in embrace, wanting this moment to lengthen into a lifetime. They touched each others faces, registering all the contours, the pimple-scars, the eyebrows, the lips, the eyes that read perfection. They whispered promises, promises that nothing would keep them apart. Dusk soon arrived and Africa and India parted, each to its separate world, unaware that the afternoon's union had borne fruit beyond the pleasure of the embrace, and the joining of spirits.

Once the young lovers had tasted the fruit of love, the forbidden fruit, nothing could keep them apart. They met on most Sundays, at the same time, at the same place, and renewed their love, their passion. Before long Julita's appetite for tamarind and lime became insatiable. And every morning she woke up weak and nauseated. Valda had noticed the changes, but she hoped that her suspicions were misguided. Knowing the consequences, she had yet to share her fears with her husband. She and her family had kept a close watch on her daughter who was already promised, so when had she found time to get pregnant and by whom? Valda refused to believe what her eyes were telling her. But finally she could no longer bear the suspense. She asked Julita, "when last you saw your period?" It was over a month ago. She asked Julita, "have you been seeing a man?" Julita, acting with shock and disbelief at such a question, replied angrily, "no." But soon she could no longer hide her secret.

The family was shamed. Julita had shamed the manhood of her father and brothers. She had committed an unthinkable crime. She was spoiled, corrupted. Her mother and father couldn't hold their heads high as they went about Forestierè and as they served their customers in their small merchandise store. They were shamed, but that could be partially remedied. The man responsible would have no choice but to marry their daughter. But then they found out that the father was black. Julita might as well have committed genocide on the family. To be pregnant before marriage was unforgivable, but to sleep with a black man was unthinkable.

This atrocity of her daughter, this shame, was worse than anything that Valda had experienced. It was worse than the cruel treatment she had received from her previous husband and mother-in-law; worse than the three months of doom, sickness, and revulsion on her trans-oceanic odyssey to this land; worse than the day of the Shipwrecked Indians; worse even than the secret she was carrying, the secret of having being raped by the eighteen-year-old son of the white owner of Forestierè Estate a month after her arrival in her new homeland.

When her daughter's abomination became apparent, Valda fell into despair. *God, when will You lay down my cross? My daugh-*

ter, my only daughter, already promised, has been bedding with this neg, this slave, like an animal in heat. These neg, these slaves, these big, black, good-for-nothing apes. These apes, good only for a good dance, a good laugh, who cannot keep a penny in their pockets even if you were to pay them to. These dumb, silly, uncivilized slaves, who would sell anything they own, spend everything they have for the sake of a good time, a good fete. These lazy, unmannerly apes, who bed with the indiscretion of dogs. What could be worse than my own daughter, my only daughter, already promised, bedding with one of them? God, why didn't you let me perish on the VOLGA?

Valda who arrived against her will as an indentured servant didn't consider that her life and the life of the other Indians on the plantation were little-better than that of slaves. True, unlike the Africans who arrived in shackles and were bonded for life, the Indians and their children were never the property of someone else. They were bonded to the plantations only for five to ten years after which they were free to return to India. True, they had been freer than the slaves to practice their Hindu and Muslim religions, to carry on their religious festivals, to uphold their music, dances and family and community way of life, to continue eating the same type of dishes they ate in India. But when it came to plantation life, there wasn't much of a difference between an indentured servant and a slave.

The day after Valda had survived the shipwreck, she had been given a thorough medical examination, weighed and measured, and deemed fit to start work. Several plantations bade on her. She went to the highest bidder—the Forestierè Estate—and signed a contract she couldn't read, the contents of which she vaguely understood from the explanation of the Indian interpreter. Two days after her arrival at Forestierè after a five-mile buggy ride and a two-mile walk, the overseer of the estate put her to work picking, piling and breaking cocoa pods. To pay her four-pence, the daily wage for children, instead of eight-pence, the wage for women, the overseer classified her a child. And though her contract called for seven hours of work per day, the estate forced her to work nine, sometimes ten hours. Fewer hours incurred a cut in pay. The plantation provided her with free housing, but the housing was an overcrowded barrack, a "coolie dwelling," no different from the "nigger yards." The estate was supposed to provide the indentured servants with free medical attention, but they only saw a doctor when they were dying, when it was too late. Mostly, they made do with bush medicine. And one had to be dying to get an excuse from work. For three months Valda was given a fixed ration of food, no more than what the slaves used to get, which cost her one-third of her four pence daily wages. Accused of laziness, at the end of some weeks she received no wages. Conditions improved slightly, when, after three months on the plantation, she got married and the overseer could no longer deny her womanhood and so changed her classification from child to woman. As a woman she started earning eight pence instead of four pence, and she and her husband started growing their own food on the plot of land the plantation allotted them and the wage deductions for the food rations ended. And a year later they built their own hut, and had a place to call their own. But the long hours of work had continued with little relief. The overseer harassed and constantly threatened them with wage cuts, withdrawal of family plots, and outright beatings. Their five-year contract ended, but no free passage back to India as promised in the contract was forthcoming. With no land of their own, little money saved, they had little choice but to continue slaving on the estate.

The estate had forced them to live a life not much different from that of slaves. Nevertheless, they had never been slaves and they had arrived with most of their culture intact. Besides, if color was the basis for division, the currency of value, of self-worth, then Indians would fall below whites but definitely above blacks. So to Valda and the other Indians, inter-marrying with blacks was to dilute their culture, their color, their value. Marrying blacks was an act of self-abasement.

Nonetheless, after a few months of shame and confusion, guilt and despair, Valda grudgingly accepted her daughter and learned to live with the shame, even though she, like most women of any society, was the bearer of the culture and tradition of her people, the very traditions her daughter's indiscretion had made a mockery of.

But the men of the family, even those who didn't live in the house any longer, couldn't forget, couldn't forgive, couldn't live with the shame Julita had brought on them. Their whole concept of self was at stake. Their manhood had come under question. They had seen what to them was the power the black skin of the "negs" emitted. They had watched the "negs'" loose, sexy strut, the abundance profligacy with which they approached life as if there were no tomorrow. They had heard stories and some of them had borne witness to the size of the "negs'" penises. It seemed to them that theirs paled in comparison. The only way they could describe the size of the "negs'" penises was to compare them with that of donkeys, supplying the men of the family with what they considered further proof that the "negs" were not much higher than animals. They had also heard stories that once an Indian woman slept with a "neg," an Indian man could never again satisfy her.

These were serious threats. Many more men than women immigrated so there was already a shortage of Indian women to wed Indian men. And since the Indians held fast to their policy of maintaining the purity of their race, out of necessity cousins were marrying cousins, five brothers of one family were marrying five sisters of a neighboring family. So besides the threat to their manhood, since the Indians were already a small minority, under three percent of the population, such indiscretions of their daughters and sisters were a threat to their very survival as a distinct race on the island.

With so much at stake the men of Forestierè had been very diligent in keeping their women away from what they considered the
insatiable appetites of the "negs." When there was a dance or a
bazaar at their village, they came ready with cutlasses to protect
their women from "contamination." But they had a difficult time
keeping some blacks away. Not with the hair of the Indian women
reaching to their buttocks, the feel of the hair coating their arms
coming to attention from a caress, their coyness, coquettishness,
their lucent eyes expressing desires waiting to be flamed, their
hidden smiles that communicated more effectively than words. It
was too much to ask. Cutlasses couldn't keep some blacks away.
Instead, they came with their own cutlasses, and fishing guns,
ready to battle for the opportunity of appeasing their appetites. So
at dances and bazaars, many a battle ensued. The Indians pro-
tected their women, their manhood, their race, with valor. After
each dance, both sides carried badges of cutlass wounds.

To Julita's father and brothers, all their bravery, their valor,
their cutlass wounds worn as tokens of their manhood, had come
to nought. So unlike Valda, the conscience of her family, the
guardian of the heritage, the tradition, the culture of her people,
Julita's father and brothers couldn't forgive her. Julita's bulging
stomach was a rope of shame tightening around their necks, suffocating their manhood, extinguishing their existence. When Julita's
father got wind of the news, undeterred by her pregnancy, he cut
her back open with a freshly cut whip from the tamarind tree from
which she had been appeasing her appetite for tartness. After that
her father and brothers would slap her around whenever their disgust for her broke out of control. Julita's name was no longer
Julita. She was a *jamet*, a *salòp*, the woman who fucks "negs."

The rest of Forestierè were no less shocked than Julita's
family. Perhaps if it had happened to some other family, the village would have been caught by surprise, but they wouldn't have
been shocked, for example, the family where the husband was
notorious for getting drunk every payday, and religiously beating

his wife and children. The same family where, if the wife didn't accompany her man every payday to pick up his pay, give him his rum money and bring the rest home, he would drink and gamble every cent of his week's wages. But Julita's family was one of the most, if not the most, respectable families of Forestierè. Even though it was a losing battle, Valda was one of the few remaining villagers who insisted that her children learn to speak Hindi. Many of the villagers had long switched from Hindu to Roman Catholic, but Valda maintained a shrine in a corner of her bedroom and would hold on to her religion until her death.

Julita's family had been a model of hard work and family togetherness. Her father was never known to beat his wife. As their sons became old enough to work, they joined their parents on the plantation. Fifteen years after they were married, the family had saved enough to set up a small grocery store which Valda attended while her husband kept working on the plantation and tending his ground-provision plot. Five years later the family bought some land bordering the plantation and soon, in addition to growing food crops, Valda's husband was rearing cows, and sheep. Not much later the family extended the grocery store into a general supply store, and Valda's husband stopped working for the plantation and started working full time tending his animals, his ground provision plots and helping Valda in the store. And now, thirty years since Valda's first husband and mother-in-law had sold her into bondage, thirty years since her arrival in the land of the gods, thirty years since her second marriage, except for Julita who was promised, her children, her six sons, were married (though the two youngest still lived at home with their wives) and following in their father's footsteps. Up until Julita's indiscretion, the family was the very symbol of hard work, family togetherness, thrift, and of upholding Indian traditions—all the things held dear by the village, by a people in an alien land. And now the daughter of this family had committed the unthinkable, the unforgivable; she who was promised to another.

So the village was shocked. Some said that Julita had too much pride. Being the baby of the family they had spoilt her. Those families who had been jealous of Julita's family laughed with scorn and said, "they are so good, so high and so holy, so prideful, but look how low they have fallen, fucking negs, slaves, animals. What will they do next, fuck their cows?" Some of Julita's friends sympathized with her in her presence, touching her bulging stomach, but behind her back they giggled and asked, "what does she see in those black apes, having vice with them? So disgusting!"

Valda's friends, the sincere ones, kept asking her, "Oh my God, Valda, what are you going to do? So disgraceful, so ungrateful, that daughter of yours! After raising her like a princess, how could she do that to you?" Her husband's friends kept telling him that he should throw his daughter out immediately, disown her. That would teach the other girls in Forestierè a lesson. Forestierè couldn't afford such indiscretions. Her sons' friends and enemies alike, those jealous of their success, taunted them, telling them that their sister was sleeping with donkeys and brutes. Her sons couldn't let such insults go unnoticed, so they were constantly getting into fights, defending their honor, their manhood.

But no amount of fighting could change the fact. Julita had shamed her family. And as Julita's child, unaware of the distress and shame her presence was causing, grew inside her mother's womb, the shame grew and the manhood of Julita's father and brothers shrank in direct proportion. Soon the shame was too much to bear. The manhood of the men of the family had shrunk to unlivable proportions. They would have to murder Julita as they would have done if they were in the hinterland of India or put her out. Out of the house, out of Forestierè, out of sight.

Meanwhile, despite all the abuse Julita was receiving, all the shame she had brought on her family, all the anguish she had caused, she continued meeting secretly with her lover, hiding the abuse as much as possible from him.

When Julita was six months pregnant the father had had

enough. He slapped her around for the last time and put her out
of the house. He told her never to set foot in his house and in this
village again or else he would kill her with his bare hands. This
was the last time that Julita's parents would see her alive. Valda,
the one sold into bondage, the one raped a month after her arrival
in her new homeland, would grieve for her daughter for the rest
of her life.

With a bundle containing her worldly possessions on her
head, Julita walked part of the way, and hitched a ride on a donkey cart the rest of the way to her lover. The lover whose parents
couldn't understand their son's fascination with Indian girls. *What
does our son see in these collies? These collies with no rhythm,
who couldn't dance to a tune even if someone were to pay them.
These collies with absolutely no taste. No taste in food, no taste
in clothing, no taste in colors. These collies who ate rice morning, noon, and evening, as if rice was going extinct. Who painted
everything pink, their house, their buggies, as if pink was the only
color left on earth. These collies who are as cheap and miserly
as only collies can be. So miserly that some of them sell their children to the devil. And when it comes to money, rum is their only
soft spot, even though they hold their liquor no better than a newly-
born babe.*

*So what is it about these collies that fascinate our boy so?
True, their women enter womanhood like blossoming roses, but
it is a short-lived beauty. Collies are weak and age fast. They don't
keep as well as blacks or even whites, for that matter. The only
thing collies have going for them is nice hair and fair skin. But
still, that shouldn't be enough to make our son ignore the many
Kwéyòl girls chasing after him, but come to attention anytime a
collie girl happens to pass by. Hasn't our son noticed that when
one marries one of these collies, one marries not just the one person but the whole family going way back to Calcutta? Worse, collies think that because they didn't arrive here in chains they are
better than us. One does well to stay away from those weak, cheap,*

drunken collies. But our son would not listen. Whatever he sees in these collies must be something.

Julita arrived six months pregnant, on a dusty Thursday afternoon, at the home of Leonce. Leonce and his father were out working in the cane fields, his three younger siblings were attending school, only his mother was at home. When his mother saw the sobbing, pregnant Indian girl enter her yard, though her son had not informed her or any one in the family of his mischief, she knew right away what had happened. Her son who would not listen to her when she told him to leave these people alone, had finally gotten himself in trouble. She knew those collies well. They would rather disown or murder their daughters than see them marrying a *Kwéyòl*. Her three-room shack could hardly hold another person, not to mention a pregnant woman. But the girl was sobbing uncontrollably, and she was carrying her son's child, her grandchild. She didn't care much for these people. They were cheap and sly, and they thought they were better than *Kwéyòls*. But she personally had nothing against them. Unlike the Indians, she didn't have a three-thousand-year-old unbroken tradition to uphold. Slavery had taken care of that. The only race she didn't care to mix with was the race that had enslaved her ancestors. Aside from that race, which she would hate to her grave, she was willing to mix with any one who was willing to mix with her. She swallowed her misgivings and took in the pregnant girl. She was thinking, we can keep her until she gives birth and is back on her feet, then both she and my son will have to leave the house. There cannot be two hens in a coop.

Julita gave birth to a girl whom Leonce named Christine and a year later they moved to Castries. Leonce wanted to stay in Babonneau, close to his parents, but Julita would have none of that. She had been so grateful to Leonce's parents for keeping her that she had been the perfect daughter-in-law. In spite of her pregnancy and in spite of the insistence of Leonce that she take it easy, she had done more than her share of the house chores. She had listened quietly and dutifully to the many insults and, sometimes, admonitions of her mother-in-law.

"Put the rice away, we're not cooking rice today. I don't understand why you all collies love rice so much. You all eat rice as if rice is going out of style. No wonder you are so thin... Put two more spoonfuls, you all collies too cheap, don't you know you have to put plenty of powder-milk when making the child's bottle? I don't want my granddaughter to grow up as thin as you... Why do you wear the same thing, the same color, all the time? Don't you have any taste? I will never understand you all collies: no taste in food, no taste in clothes... I don't understand why collies are so cruel, how could they put you out six months pregnant? They didn't want any *Kwéyòl* blood in their family, did they? They thought my son wasn't good enough for you, eh? Well, well, well, see where you are now. You sure have all the *Kwéyòl* you can handle... Isn't it true that you all sell your children to the devil? I bet the way things turned out your parents wished they had sold you when you were small and still a virgin. I hear the devil only takes virgins... I also hear you all sing and pray to the devil in a strange language. I hope you people haven't placed any of that *calcutta maho péma* nonsense on my son, because if you all have, you all will know what our black magic and our obeah is all about..."

After eighteen months of such unanswered talk, Julita wanted to put distance between herself and her mother-in-law. She also wanted to put further distance between herself and her family than the four miles between Babonneau and Forestierè, because if her brothers were to catch her unawares they were likely to beat her or even murder her. Castries seemed a good answer. In Castries, as she told Leonce, he could find work in the Cul-de-Sac Valley Sugar Plantation or on the Castries wharf, and she, having learnt something about business from helping her mother in the store, could set up stall on the wharf where she could sell fishcake, bakes, roti, dalpouwi and juices to the sailors, the chabonniers, and the stevedores. Leonce had objected, but only mildly. He was too occupied with being a father. The concept was still novel to him, and he was still getting used to the idea that the woman he worshiped was his, all his. So when his love brought up the idea of moving to Castries, the city the gods hated, he objected, but only to the point that his new-found manhood, his new-found status of the head of the family demanded.

6

It was Christmas Eve night. A few hours earlier, in the early evening, chantenwellers had passed from neighborhood to neighborhood reminding the people that Christmas wasn't just about feting but about goodwill and the birth of the Messiah. Where the chantenwellers left off, radios carried on the message of hope and goodwill. Cupboards were filled with Coca-Cola, Juicy, Fanta, cider, white rum, Mount Gay Rum. Goats, sheep, and hogs tied unto house posts awaited sacrifice first thing in the morning. Houses were crowded with visiting relatives, some not seen in twenty, thirty years; some thought long dead. They had returned from abroad, England and America, mainly, to catch a bit of fire, to catch a bit of fellowship, to measure the distance they have traveled, to convince themselves that immigrating was worth the humiliation of second class citizenry. So houses were full of people, full of laughter, full of measuring up, full of voices chatting through the night, and plenty of presents, dollars, and pounds and shillings were going around. But come midnight, the people, that is those who professed to be Roman Catholic, dressed up in their Sunday best and headed for church to attend the Christmas Eve midnight mass. Before the feting officially began, homage must be paid to the One Whose birth called for so much happiness. The house of Colletta had no visiting relatives. But the church was her family, and mass her lifeblood. As with past Christmas Eve masses, she was one of the first to arrive at the cathedral to welcome the birth of the Redeemer.

Despite the season of goodwill, the contagious spirit of giving that permeated the air, the chantenwellers' message of love and good tidings, and the Christmas carols flowing from radios in every house that could afford one, on this Christmas Eve fifteen-year-old Robert harbored nothing but ill and hatred toward the world. This night his malevolence was directed at none other than the woman who was one of the first to welcome the annual coming of the Messiah.

Next to Felina, Colletta was the one he most hated. Throughout the years he had noticed how, when their paths crossed, she looked at him as if he were Satan Himself. How her right hand moved to hold on to the crucifix cross she always carried around her neck, and how she always mumbled what seemed to him a curse. She was always telling on him, bringing reports to his mother. He could still remember that she was the one who had told his mother about his shirley biscuit escapade at M&C. Once, he overheard her telling the neighbors that he was cursed, and if he didn't end up on the gallows, he would surely end up in jail. When she saw him coming, her mouth clamped tight, her hand moved instinctively to her cross, and she stared at him with eyes filled with ill-will. As the years passed, his hatred for her hardened into something akin to his hatred for his mother. So this Christmas Eve, as the cathedral bell signaled the commencement of the midnight mass, Robert, unwillingly accompanied by his bosom friend, sought retribution on the woman who had become his nemesis.

This wasn't the first time Robert had sought revenge on Colletta. Colletta had a black cat named Lucy, known to the whole neighborhood on account of how much care and attention she lavished on it. All the adults knew that Lucy was more than a pet to

Colletta. Lucy was a substitute for the children Colletta never had. To the then twelve-year-old Robert, the cat looked just as menacing as its owner; it seemed to stare at him with the same degree of distrust and ill-will. In some vague sense he thought that by getting rid of the cat he would get rid of both the cat and its owner. So with a piece of fried tuna he lured the cat into a flour sack, quickly tied the open end with wire, smashed the cat to pulp with a homemade cricket bat, and dumped the bag on a garbage heap. Since that day, soon after a neighbor told Robert's mother on him, the neighbor's cat or dog would be missing or the animals came home bleeding and hobbling.

But on this Christmas Eve night, what Robert had in mind was more damaging to the victim, but more beneficial to him, or so he thought, than the killing of a pet.

By now everyone in the immediate neighborhood knew that Colletta didn't bank her money. Except for the Roman Catholic Church, Colletta had a deep distrust for institutions, both government and business. She didn't join organizations. To her, banks were a way rich people had of getting their hands into the pockets of poor people. And in some vague sense she thought banks were instruments of the devil. Didn't Christ Himself chastise the money lenders who chose no other place than his temple to carry on with their abomination? So Colletta kept her life savings hidden somewhere in her house, much like in the old days when people hid their gold coins in clay jars in the bosom of the earth. Before her husband passed away three years ago, he would beg her to go and bank her money. She would earn interest. Besides, a fire or a thief could pass by and her money could go up in flames or in the pocket of a stranger.

But Colletta paid her husband no mind. Instead, after his death, she withdrew all of his savings and added it to her hidden treasure. Ironically, in spite of Colletta's aversion to banks she herself became a neighborhood bank. Knowing that Colletta had a ready stash of cash, had no children, and that her only pleasures in life were attending mass, gossiping, and deciding which among the neighborhood children were on their way to becoming criminals, it was to her that women of the neighborhood came to borrow money, to make ends meet when their husband or boyfriend was out of a job, when school was opening and their children needed school uniforms and books, or when it was First Communion and their children needed white cotton frocks and cotton stockings. When they came to her doorstep, that is, those she thought were keeping their child along the straight and narrow path, she disappeared into her one-bedroom house and returned with the exact amount requested, never displaying any more money than was necessary. Unlike the banks she despised, she didn't require interest. Her only loan condition was that her customers specify the exact day upon which they would return her money.

This was the woman, the neighborhood's loan agent, at whom, in this season of goodwill, Robert was directing his malevolence. In the afternoon, a few hours before the chantenwellers came out, he had sought the help of Trevor to execute his midnight assault. Christine greeted his arrival. She was expecting a suitor with whom she intended to hang out all night. The midnight mass wasn't for her; she had her own way of welcoming the Messiah. She stood in the door as if guarding her house against evil. Robert looked up, saw her low- heeled, white shoes, her ankles, her slender, coconut-oil-glistening legs, the curvature of her inner thighs, the edge of her red miniskirt, her pointed breasts that seemed to want to pierce her blouse, the questioning, slightly parted lips, the Indian nose, the eyes that said whatever one wished it to say, the *douglah* hair flowing free.

Since that first day of the school year, when he first laid eyes on Christine and befriended her son as a substitute for her, he seized every opportunity to visit Trevor in the hope of laying eyes on the woman he wished was his mother. Each time his eyes met hers he would stand upright and still as in a trance.

Christine never said much to him. She was uncomfortable

with the way he stared at her. His stare seemed to be saying more than what a young boy should be saying to a woman. Many times their eyes would lock in silence, and it was Trevor that would come and break the spell. Christine never imagined the power she had over Robert. She didn't know that Robert would have done whatever she asked of him. Christine was probably one of the few people that could have put Robert back on the straight and narrow path that Colletta talked so much about. A few words from Christine, a bit of attention, a return of a little of the love and admiration Robert's stare emitted, would have succeeded where Felina's merciless punishment had failed so miserably. One encouraging word, one look of compassion, a pat on the back, a rub of the head, and Robert may have cried and told her about his hatred of his mother, the cruelty, his lost father, his almost uncontrollable urge to hurt someone, to hit out at the world. And this might have been the beginning of Robert's healing.

If Robert had ever been to church, he would have realized that the way he felt each time he met Christine, and their eyes locked in this dance ritual, was the same way people felt—the lightness of being, the glowing feeling of love—after mass, after a good sermon, after a revival meeting. After each time Robert met Christine he felt like going and repent of his cruelties and changing the course of his life. Of course that feeling never lasted long. Christine who didn't have time for her own son had far less time for Robert whose eyes were asking more than she cared to give. She never said more than a few words to Robert. So as soon as Robert returned home and encountered the hatred of his mother, whatever feeling of redemption he had gained quickly dissipated.

Given his plans for the night, and knowing the effect Christine had on him, today was one of the few times that Robert didn't want to run into Christine. He was afraid that if he were to look into the eyes that held so much magic for him, he would lose heart, and not be able to carry out his punishment, his vengeance, on the woman he despised as strongly as he was enchanted by

Christine. But there she was blocking the entrance of the house, filling his view, filling his world.

At fifteen he no longer wished for her to be his mother. But something else was beginning to happen. Looking into her eyes, he felt weak, and something hardened and throbbed between his legs. He felt naked. Suddenly he was a child caught with his hands in a jar of guava-cheese. He looked into her eyes, unable to divert his stare.

She returned his stare, not smiling, giving away nothing: no encouragement, no contempt. Her matching stare stifled any flirting smile, any boldness on his part. As many times before, she stirred in him the part that was good, the deep down part, the part in all of us that has remained untouched, the child-part that wanted to be loved, to be desired, to please, to cooperate, to conform, to do the right thing.

He too stirred something in her, some primordial passion she refused to acknowledge. But the single bead of sweat that trickled from between her legs and caused her to change stance so as to trap the sweat and prevent it from rolling all the way down her legs was proof enough. She wasn't quite sure why, even when Robert was a mere child, he made her feel so uncomfortable, so confused, so stifled. She who was born with a knowledge of men. Maybe it was his wild eyes, his rawness, his coal-black skin, his lean, fat-free body which at fifteen had already taken the proportions of the body of a man. As Robert grew older the uncomfortable, tingling, stifling sensation she felt grew more pronounced.

She had seen the way he behaved when not in her presence. At the conscious level, she despised his uncouthness, his vulgarity, his unkempt self, and wondered what her son saw in him. She would have been surprised to find out that what Robert saw in her son was her. It was only the confusion caused by the subconscious stirring that he unleashed in her that prevented her disdain of him from registering in her eyes and facial expression when he gazed into her eyes.

They only stared into each other for a few seconds before Trevor came and broke the trance, but to them their stares had lasted much longer.

Christine moved back into the house.

"What's up?" greeted Trevor.

"Yeah, yeah," replied Robert, his mind following Christine into the house. He was having second thoughts about punishing Colletta. Suddenly, he wasn't feeling revengeful anymore; not after looking into the eyes of the woman he once wished was his mother. He was feeling love, forgiveness; hope, redemption. The Christmas spirit was slowly breaking through. But then he started doing what had become second nature to him—digging for the hatred in him. He fought the good feelings, he forced himself to focus on the indiscretions of Colletta: telling his mother on him, telling everyone he would end up on the gallows, putting curses on him, holding her cross every time he passed her. "I will show her, I will show her," he mumbled. "Is jail she say I going, is hang she say I go hang, then tonight I will show her, in her fucking ass. I will give she a taste of she own prophecy."

"What? Who you talking about?" asked Trevor.

"Yeah, partner, I have a plan to make us plenty of Christmas money. And at the same time we will show Colletta, the witch, the *souse* who never minds her own business, a lesson she will never forget.

"The cruel witch is always telling my mother on me. Once when my mother was beating me, I saw the witch looking out of her window, smiling at me. But guess what partner, she doesn't bank her money. All the money she makes from selling is hidden right there in her house. And I hear that her husband left her plenty of money. Tonight we go make the witch pay for not minding her own stinking business. Tonight go be our pay day. She never misses mass. Don't talk for Christmas Eve mass. So when the clock strikes midnight, we go get some of that money."

As soon as Robert said "plan," Trevor became wary. He had

plenty of reasons to be cautious. While one half of his mind followed Robert's talk, the other half dwelt on the many reasons why he should be on his guard. Robert's plans, or devilments, as Trevor often thought of them, were invariably about stealing or finding some way to lay his hands on girls, and he, Trevor, usually got the raw end of these devilments.

Like the day they went up the Morne to steal ripe bananas at the home of one of the managers of the Banana Growers' Association. The man's house, down a slope overlooking the Cul-de-Sac Valley, stood on tall pillars. Under the house he always had hanging several bunches of ripening bananas. One mid-afternoon, when Robert was sure that no one was home, he led Trevor to the house. Once under the house, they each quickly detached a hand of yellowish-ripe bananas, a few fingers breaking off the hand. Just when they were about to retrace their steps, a bulldog, nostrils flaring, saliva streaming, teeth snarling, came charging. Robert, holding tight to his spoils, ran, and in one bound leapt over the fence. Trevor wasn't as lucky. Letting go of his bananas, he grabbed the fence to climb over, but he was too late. The dog jumped, and his jaws closed on Trevor's buttocks. Trevor yanked himself over the fence, catching his fall on his hands. Robert started laughing. As if by design, the dog had bitten a clean, round patch out of Trevor's pants, leaving his teeth marks, like a signature, on Trevor's bare behind. By then Trevor had wet himself.

Or like that other time on Vigie Beach, not too far from Latoc Hotel. It was around four o'clock on a Saturday afternoon, the beach empty save for a few strolling tourists and the occasional local. After a long swim Robert and Trevor were relaxing on the beach when a tourist woman, hair turning grey, a bag swinging on her shoulders, came strolling by. She had probably just arrived on the island; she had no tan, her skin was white and pale. "Partner, here comes some easy money," Robert said. Then he walked up to the woman and asked for the time. As the woman turned her eyes toward her watch, Robert yanked her bag from her shoulders and ran. Trevor, the fool that he was, ran, trying to catch up with his friend, as if he were part of the theft. The woman shouted for help and one of Latoc Hotel's security guards came out of the sea-almond shade and gave chase. He caught up with Trevor, tripped and pinned him to the ground, Trevor's face pressed into the sand. Robert got away. The security guard was just about to put some serious blows on Trevor, when the tourist caught up and said that the guard had caught the wrong one. Still, the guard cursed and slapped Trevor a few times. All this was for nothing. Except for women things, the tourist's bag had nothing—no jewelry, no money.

And a few weeks ago, a girl nearly scratched out Trevor's eyes. In the same way that Trevor was wary of Robert's devilments, the girls in Robert's neighborhood were wary of him. At a younger age, when the neighborhood children played hide and seek in the early evening, some girl always returned from hiding shedding tears. Robert's self-appointed reward for finding his quarry was to force his hands between her legs, and, when the girls began to grow bosoms, grabbing their breast. Soon, when Robert was around, the girls refused to play hide and seek. Now, it wasn't that the other boys didn't pet the girls, fondling them as much as they were allowed to get away with. After all, this was the fun of playing hide and seek, and for the most part the girls looked forward to playing. But Robert never sought or received the girls' implicit agreement, and his poking between the girls' legs, or his grabbing of their breasts, seemed more to inflict pain and punishment than the clumsiness of boys exploring the secrets of the female anatomy. The girls also learned to beware of Robert when sea-bathing. He would sneak up on them under water, and give them the same treatment that he gave them when they played hide and seek. So as soon as Robert entered the water and headed toward the girls, they quickly exchanged water for dry land.

With Trevor it was a different story. The girls usually surrounded him, teasing, jumping on his back, playing canoe with him.

To them, being with Trevor was just like being with another girl. He was shy, sensitive, and pretty as a girl. They were able to use Trevor to practice getting to know boys, while avoiding the accompanying costs. So like duck hunters using artificial ducks to draw in live ducks, Robert used Trevor to get to the girls. He would wait some distance away from Trevor, let the girls gather around him, and then, while they were preoccupied with Trevor, he would move soundlessly, mostly under water, toward the girls. His surprised victim would scream, and like a herd of deer one of whose members has been snatched by a lion, the girls would scamper to land. It was during one such raid, a couple of weeks ago, that a girl nearly scratched out Trevor's eyes. Robert's submarine assault caused the girl so much pain, that like an angry tigress, she instinctively clawed the face of Trevor, the only male she saw in her blinded rage. Robert had slipped away.

After many such episodes, Trevor was deeply wary of Robert's insatiable urge for devilment. Remembering this last escapade of Robert's, Trevor's right hand moved instinctively to the facial mark left by the girl's rage.

"You must be mad, or what? I eh going to jail for nobody. From the time we small you always getting me in one kind of trouble or the other. Just week before last you nearly make that girl take out my eyes. See, her fingernails' marks are still on my face. And now you want to steal the old woman's money. You really need to see a brain doctor."

"Partner that woman full of money, and she doesn't have anyone to spend it on. She goes nowhere. She only goes to church. We eh go take all her money. We'll just take fifty dollars or so. She eh go even miss that. Besides, that serves her right for interfering in what is none of her business."

"No way. I eh go follow you in jail. I eh spending my Christmas in jail."

"You beginning to sound just like Colletta. Who say you going to jail? Partner, you don't have to go in the house. All I want you to do is keep watch, and whistle three times if anyone catch wind of what is going on. Besides, there eh go be anybody around. Everybody will be at mass. And if they catch us, it's only I that will be punished, because it is I who enter the house and take the money. Besides, we too young to go to jail. You safe, partner. You have nothing to worry about."

Trevor was silent, and Robert knew he had him. It was the same each time. Robert came up with his scheme. Trevor objected strongly at first. Then Robert made it appear that the intended victims deserved whatever he had in store for them and that the victims could afford it, or would not even feel the consequences, and then he downplayed the risk of being caught, and if caught, he softened the punishment.

Robert's begging tone of voice, his humble posture, as he went about convincing Trevor to come along with him, gave Trevor the impression that Robert desperately needed him, that without him Robert could do nothing, was nothing. It was the same each time Robert felt the urge to strike out, to hurt someone. He made it look like he had to have Trevor with him, like he had to have at least one witness to record his deeds. Trevor didn't harbor hatred, he didn't have an inner need to lash out, but each time he got swallowed up in Robert's need of him. To receive so much attention, to be needed so strongly, was exhilarating. This was what Trevor had an inner need for. Besides, Robert had become his big brother, his protector, his compass. The one who stood up for him against the world, the one that gave his life form and direction.

Like that day, several years ago, when he and Robert were playing football at Vigie. After the game a boy from Lancers, on the opposite team, the losing team, came up in his face, calling his mother a *jamet*. Trevor, the boy who avoided fights at all cost, who had no inherent urge to lash out at the world, suddenly lunged at his antagonist, striking in rage. Still he was no match for the boy from Lancers who was three years his senior. Soon after the initial shock of the attack, the boy from Lancers had him pinned to the ground and was raising his fist to teach Trevor a lesson. Just as quickly as the fight began, Robert came to the rescue. He kneed the adversary in the back, yanked him off Trevor, and proceeded to smother him with punches. The boy from Lancers, a year older than Robert, cried shamelessly in surrender. Robert didn't heed his cry, he was lashing at, not just the boy, but his mother, Colletta, his father that refused to show up, the world. It had taken four of the other Conway boys to get Robert off the bruised and bleeding boy from Lancers. That day the boy from Lancers found out the hard way what the boys from Conway and those attending the same school with Robert and Trevor already knew. That to mess with Trevor, was to invite Robert to the party.

Trevor had not only to be thankful to Robert for protecting him from the fists of bullies. Shortly after his eleventh birthday, Robert saved him from a death by water. They were swimming and frolicking in the Choc Bay area. Several beach parties were going on, so there were plenty of people around, but very few were in the water. Most were drinking, eating, dancing, having a good time. Trevor swam ahead of Robert, daring him into a race. Suddenly he disappeared. A few months before, a large yacht had come too close to shore and had run aground, leaving a depression on the sea bed. The depression which had created a circular current was at the very spot where Trevor had momentarily stopped to look back to see if Robert was up to racing. The current had pulled Trevor into the depression. At first Robert thought Trevor had dived to see if he could touch sand. They often competed on who could come up with sand at various depths. But when Trevor didn't surface within the amount of time it should have taken him to grab sand and come back up, Robert dived after him. He searched the bottom of the sea, but saw no trace of Trevor. He came up for air, swam a little bit ahead, and dived again. When he was about to come back for air, he saw something a short distance ahead that could be Trevor, but he had to come up for air. He took a few gulps of air and went down again. On his way down he got caught in the current. It swirled him around, pulling him down. He momentarily lost his sense of direction. Then his feet touched something. He fought the current and felt for what was down there. He felt something like an arm. He grabbed on to the arm, hooked his left arm around Trevor's upper body, just under the shoulders, and headed for air, clawing water with his right arm and pushing up with his legs. He was only thirteen but his body was almost man-size and he had the strength of an eighteen year old. Still, when he surfaced he was panting for air, and was exhausted, as if he were the one drowning. Gulping for air, he moved doggedly, holding on to his friend, now unconscious, toward the beach, toward land. Slowly, his friend was slipping from his grasp. Lucky for him, when he had gone half the distance to shore, some of the people on the beach saw his life and death struggle. Several of the men rushed into the water, and swam quickly to Robert's aid. The men carried both the rescuer and the rescued to shore. If not for Robert's holding on to Trevor, the men would have been unable to figure out which one was drowning and which was the savior. On the beach the rescue was far from over. Trevor was barely alive. The two men who were pressing Trevor's stomach, and breathing into his mouth were just about to give up hope when sea-water gushed out of Trevor's mouth and he began breathing again. After that day the already inseparable friends became even more so.

So despite Trevor's misgivings, as in the past, he found it impossible to let down the friend that needed him so much, that paid him so much attention, many times more than did his own mother, the friend that had become his protector, his savior, his big brother, his de facto father, the friend that had saved his life.

"O.K. But I eh going inside the house, and if anyone catch you, I eh sticking around. I eh going to follow you in jail."

"Partner, you safe, this is going to be the best and richest Christmas you go ever have," said Robert, embracing his friend. Trevor pushed him away, smiling, in spite of his foreboding.

7

Midnight. Christmas Eve. The church bells ushered in the Messiah. The last of the mass-goers had hurried out of the Conway and had the church in their sights. Engulfed in a blue darkness, the Conway, save for croaking toads and the occasional dog barking, was quiet. Trevor was standing in the alley, keeping watch. With flashlight in hand, his shadow looked furtively in both directions and crept through a hole in the rust-red, zinc-patched fence. Staying low, he moved swiftly toward the backdoor of the one-bedroom shack. A few feet from the door he tripped over a white pail of soaking clothes. He broke the fall on the palm of his hands, the flashlight straying, stones digging into the flesh of his palms, the stench of the outhouse filling his nostrils. "Mother cunt," he softly hissed. Until he entered the house he could not switch on the flashlight; a passerby might see the light. He groped for the flashlight and straightened up. Holding the door's bottom edge, he pulled, causing the door flaps to come apart and expose the cross bar that locked the door from inside. He slid his hand through the gap between the door flaps and forced the bar up and out of its hooks. The bar fell to the floor, making a noise magnified by the quiet of the night. He froze momentarily, his left hand moving instinctively to his throat. Forewarned, mice escaped the house through holes in the floor. The moment passed. He switched on his flashlight and entered the house. The floor boards squeaked. He went straight into the bedroom which to him smelled of old people. This house smells like a witch, he is thinking. He looked under the ageless wooden-framed bed, the flashlight making a rainbow of the dust particles. Under the bed, worn out shoes and a grip with mice-bitten holes. He pulled out the grip, ripped it open, and found spools of thread, a rusted pair of scissors, scattered coins, sewing needles, nothing of value. Disgusted, he slid the grip back under the bed, and then raised the coconut-fibre mattress, only old bedding under it. Then with expectancy, he pulled out the drawers of the dresser that seemed of an earlier century. There were only clothes and more things of no value to him. His flashlight picked out two night soil vases tipped upside-down in a corner of the room. He lifted them. They hid nothing. He left the bedroom and entered the only other room in the house, the room that other than sleeping served all functions of the house— entertaining, dining, and cooking when rain precluded cooking outside. Not too many hiding places there. A cabinet that held the woman's treasured dishes and glassware, some of which dated back to her grandmother's wedding, was the only thing that offered itself for search. Getting desperate, he swept the dishes aside, and searched the cabinet thoroughly. Caught by surprise, cockroaches scuttled for cover. The cabinet yielded nothing, so he returned to the bedroom and flashed his flashlight around the room. In a corner of the room he noticed a pile of clothes awaiting laundry, the only place he hasn't searched. He dug into the clothes, his hands hit something hard, it was a trunk. He tried to open the trunk, but it was locked. He went to the other room for a knife. Quickly, he cut a large hole in the trunk and pulled out its contents—a couple of wedding dresses, some dresses long out of fashion, and some men's clothes. Then his hands hit something more solid than clothes. He pulled it up. It was an old pillow case, and inside were bundles of dollar bills. "I well catch you, witch," he whispered with a smile. "Now see who laughs last." He wrapped the top of the pillow case in his right hand and stepped out of the house, closing the door behind him, soundlessly. At the fence he looked in both directions and crept through the hole and onto the alley. He joined Trevor. Quietly, they walked the night to their destination— the remains of a house burnt down a couple of months after it was built. Laying eyes on the ashes of his dreams, the owner, an expatriate living in England who was planning to resettle in St. Lucia, cursed Castries and vowed to die in England. So the house was never rebuilt, and bush now grew inside. At the burnt house, Robert stuffed the money into a large empty powdered-milk can, and slid the can under the bush at the base of one of the still standing stone and mortar pillars. An opossum scurried away from the commotion.

Christmas came. And late morning some of the neighborhood children, those who were in Colletta's good graces, came to wish her Merry Christmas. Childless, it was Colletta's Christmas tradition to give each child, depending on their age, ten cents, twenty-five cents, fifty cents, seventy-five cents, and sometimes even a dollar for Christmas. So weeks before Christmas, the children had been delighting in the sweeties, the chewing gums, the tablets, and the matinees on which they would spend their Christmas money. Throughout the year they had made sure to greet Colletta with extra respect and had taken careful heed of her constant chastisement. Today was their payday.

"Good morning, Miss Colletta, Merry Christmas," the children chorused.

Deep in sleep, Colletta heard the chorus as from afar. And for a while she thought she was still at the midnight mass, and the voices the church choir. She was thinking, I fell asleep. I never fall asleep in church.

"Merry Christmas, Miss Colletta," the children again chorused. Still half asleep, Colletta opened her bedroom window and saw the group of waiting children.

"What you all doing here so early?" She asked. The children looked down at their toes. "Go home, all of you." The children shuffled their feet in disappointment.

Colletta looked on top of her dresser at the ageless mechanical clock which once belonged to her mother. It was ten o'clock. She was usually up by six. But last night she had returned home close to two o'clock. After mass, she and a group of other parishioners had stuck around, sharing gossip. When she got home, she was so tired and sleepy that she hadn't bothered to light her lamp. She had changed into her night dress in the dark and fell asleep almost immediately. She hadn't noticed that her mattress was slightly out of place, that two of her dresser drawers were halfway drawn, and that the clothes on the trunk awaiting laundry were scattered.

When she saw the time, she told the children to wait. The children stopped and turned around, expectancy returning to their eyes. Then Colletta started to notice that something was amiss. Her two night-soil vases were upturned, her wedding dress mingled with the dirty clothes on the trunk, her kitchen knife half-buried in the clothes. Her heart began to hammer loud and fast. She went quickly to the trunk and saw a large hole. She unlocked the trunk, and frantically searched for her lifetime savings, her retirement, the children's Christmas, but found nothing. She removed all the clothes from the trunk, but nothing.

"My God, my God, it's gone, it's all gone," she murmured. And then the waiting children heard a scream that froze them in space and time, and brought Sophia, Cora and two other neighborhood women, Lydia and Eldora, running, forgetting their Christmas pots on the coalpots.

The women knocked urgently on the front door, but Colletta didn't respond. They tried the back door. It was open. They hurried into Colletta's bedroom. She was seated on the bed, her face in her hands, her body rocking back and forth. She didn't look up, but she kept mumbling, "It's gone, it's gone."

"What's gone?" asked Cora.

"Everything. It's all gone, everything is gone, it's all over."

"Is it your money?" Asked Sophia, remembering that Colletta didn't bank her money.

"It's gone, all of it is gone."

"My God!" said Lydia, whom, just last week, Colletta had loaned money to tide her over the holiday season.

The women held Colletta like they would a child in distress. They told her not to worry. In less than no time the police would catch the thieves. But all the while the women kept wondering who could have stolen the woman's money and they pondered the immensity of the crime. This had never happened before. No one had ever broken in someone's house in the Conway, definitely not on Christmas Eve night. What is this world coming to?

"I know who did it, I know who did it," mumbled Colletta.

"What? Who? Who?"

Colletta suddenly raised her head from her hands, her eyes sharp and piercing as if responding to an insult. "That cursed Felina boy, of course. Who else? Who else? That boy was born cursed and his whole generation is cursed. Why you think the landslide buried his mother's family alive? And why you think his grandmother died choking on her own blood?"

"No Colletta," said Sophia, "true that boy is rotten, and will probably end up a vagabond. But he is only fifteen. No fifteen-year-old would be bold enough to break into somebody's house and steal all their money. This was done by seasoned professionals. In fact, I wouldn't be surprised if later today we hear that several other places were robbed last night."

"Sophia, I'm old enough to be your mother, so listen to me. I can sniff criminals, those heading for jail or the gallows, from miles away. When I say that boy is cursed, he is cursed. That boy is a born criminal. Don't you remember that before the boy could barely talk he went and stole M&C's shirley biscuits? Cora, remember not long before that he stole your pennies when he came to pick up his mother's dress? And don't tell me you all haven't realized that soon after you all tell the boy's mother about his none ending wickedness, your dogs or cats disappear, or they come home bloody. How about my cat, Lucy, which disappeared into thin air? What do you think happened to it?"

The women remembered. They remembered the savage beatings Felina laid on the boy each time he was caught in mischief. They remembered the boy always fighting: at standpipes, at school, on the playing field; fighting while playing football, cricket, marbles, and tops. They could not count the number of times they had warned their children to stay clear of the boy. "He is nothing but trouble," they would tell their children. And they remembered their missing dogs and cats, and those that came home so damaged that they had to put them to sleep. But it had never occurred to the women that the boy was the culprit. True, the boy was a menace to the neighborhood, but it was still difficult for them to believe that the boy had stolen the woman's lifetime savings.

Suddenly, Colletta started laughing, startling the women. "I have always told you all that boy will end up in jail or the gallows. Well, see, see, see. I'm going to have him locked up before the day is over." She laughed again. "He is going to spend the rest of his Christmas in jail." She got up suddenly, startling the women a second time. "Give me room. Give me room for me to put on my clothes. I'm going straight to the police station."

The women left, baffled about how the despondent, lifeless Colletta had suddenly sprung to life. They were all a bit unsure of her sanity. As soon as they were out of the house, Sophia said, "but who could have stolen the woman's money? The woman has no husband, and day and night, rain or sunshine, the woman is by the road, by the cinema, selling, trying to make a living, and you mean to tell me a good for nothing son-of-a-bitch passed by on no other night but Christmas Eve and steal all the woman's money."

"Colletta should be the last person someone should do that to." said Lydia. "She is always there to give a helping hand. With six kids, and a husband who is in and out of work, I don't know how I would have gotten through this holiday season without the money she lent me. In fact, I don't know of anyone in this neighborhood who could honestly say that Colletta hasn't lent them a helping hand."

"You are so right," said Sohia. "When my mother died several years ago it was Colletta who loaned me some of the money I needed for the funeral."

"I don't understand people now-a-days," said Cora. "They have no respect for others' property. I don't know what the world is coming to. I tell you, we are living on borrowed time."

"Don't get me wrong," said Eldora, "I feel deeply sorry for Colletta. But let's face it, that woman is just too hard headed for her own good. She just refused to put her money in the bank. You all know that she and her husband used to quarrel all the time about that. True, that boy of Felina's is wicked, but Colletta is always yapping about him, how he evil, how he curse, how he this, how he that. And now she is accusing him of stealing her money. The way she gets on the boy's case, you would think he has killed her mother or something. Isn't Felina's merciless beatings punishment enough?"

"How can hatred beget love?" said Cora. "It is obvious as night and day that Felina hates the boy. As if it was the boy's fault that his father abandoned her. Hatred begets only hatred. What that boy needs is love and caring, the gentle love of Jesus."

"Cora, I think that boy has passed the point of no return," said Lydia. "He is a lost cause. Not even God's hands can straighten him out. He may not be the one who stole the money, but sooner or later that boy will get himself in trouble with the law. I, for one, make sure my children stay clear of him."

"How can you say such a thing?" said Cora. " Don't you know that until the spirit of God has left someone, there is no such thing as a lost cause? The Bible says: *Though your sins be as scarlet, they shall be as white as snow.* If Christ could turn the prostitute, Mary Magdalene, and the Christian Killer, Paul of Damascus, around, He can surely turn around a mere boy."

"Amen," said Sophia.

As the women left the yard and entered the walk path, neighbors standing in doorways or looking through windows were shouting "What happen to Colletta?" The news traveled fast and wide. Colletta's neighbors received the news in great detail: the cutup trunk, the wedding dresses mixed with dirty clothes, Colletta reduced first to senility and then to insanity. Those from afar, beyond the Conway, heard only that on Christmas Eve night someone broke into the house of an old widow and stole her life's savings.

True to her word, at eleven-thirty, Colletta returned with a policeman. By then goats, sheep, and hogs were no longer tied onto house posts. Already offered as sacrifice to the birth of the Messiah, they were entering their final cooking stages, suffocating the Conway with a riot of culinary aromas. In every home children's mouths were watering in anticipation.

"How can you be sure it is the boy who stole your money? Did anybody see him hanging around your house?" asked the policeman, yet again.

"You think I would lie on the boy. Ask anybody around here how wicked that boy is. Did you know that some time ago the boy killed my cat? And ever so often a neighbor's cat or dog comes home bloody and crippled, or worst, is missing, never to be seen again?"

"Did you or anybody see him kill your cat?"

"No, but I don't need anyone to tell me that he did it. The way he looks at me with hatred tells the whole story. That boy was born cursed, and if you don't watch it, one of these days he is going to murder somebody."

Colletta and the policeman approached Felina's house. She was carrying a pot from the coalpot outside to her kitchen. The pot was filled with a mixture of steaming beef broth and dumplings. She put down the pot, her face moist with perspiration.

"Miss, I would like to ask your son a few questions about his whereabouts last night," said the policeman, tall and erect.

"Which son? What for?"

"Robert, of course," said Colletta.

"Is this about your money, Colletta?"

"You damn right it is, and that cursed boy of yours is going to jail." The policeman gave Colletta a stern look. She lowered her gaze, murmured something inaudible, and kept quiet.

"Robert," called Felina.

Robert had heard the arrival of Colletta and the policeman. For a second he was thinking of escaping through a window. But that would imply I am guilty, he thought.

"Where were you last night between twelve and two?" asked the policeman.

In the few seconds it took Robert to answer, his right hand moved involuntarily to his throat, and he briefly massaged it as if it were sore. This was what Felina was watching for. This gesture was a fool-proof clue that the boy was guilty. When she saw the hand move to the throat, she began thinking: so you are the one who stole the woman's money. *Salòp. Bouwo*, heartless. Then you are more evil than your father. Well, well. I will have my piece of mind, after all. I'm going to make sure they lock you up for good. With that thought, Felina lost interest in the police interrogation. She had already formulated a plan. She was going to play a cat and mouse game.

Robert stuck with the alibi he and Trevor had agreed upon.

"I and Trevor went to the movies at eight-thirty and left there sometime after one. Then I came straight home." The police looked at Felina.

"I don't know when the boy came in last night. By ten o'clock my doors were locked. He must have climbed in through his bed-room window. I'm tired of telling that doltish brother of his not to open the window for the *salòp,*" said Felina. The policeman's gaze shifted from son to mother and back to son.

"Where does that boy Trevor live?" he asked. Robert gave him directions.

"Don't think you are off the hook," said the policeman. "I'm going to be watching you like a bulldog."

"Is that all?" asked Colletta. "Aren't you going to arrest him?"

"What for?" asked the policeman.

"What for? Do you think this is a joke? What kind of police-man are you? The boy stole all my money and all what you can say is that he isn't off the hook. When do you all arrest some-body? After they have killed someone?"

The police walked off without paying Colletta further mind. Colletta stared at Robert and Felina, her eyes burning red.

Before going to see Trevor, the policeman questioned sev-eral of the neighbors. But no one had seen anything suspicious. Some were at mass, others were too busy welcoming the season to have been aware of the in and outs of the neighborhood.

Christine answered the knock of the policeman. "Yes?"

At the sight of Christine the policeman's eyes widened. She was barefoot, wearing red shorts and a man's shirt. Her hair was loose and flowed all over her face. She was yet to prepare herself for the afternoon and evening of merriment that was to come. To the policeman she was fresh, unspoiled, natural. He was a kid again, staring upon wonderment. He remained speechless for sev-eral embarrassing seconds. Then his training and professionalism surfaced. He cleared his throat of whatever was caught there, per-spiration beginning to form on his forehead. "Miss, I would like to ask your son a few questions." He cleared his throat again.

"Trevor," called Christine. She threw a questioning look at the policeman, the smile that his discomfort had provoked beginning to fade from her face.

This was one of the few times that the policeman hated his job. Oh how I would like to meet her under different circumstances, he was thinking.

"Miss, someone broke into the house of a woman down the road, a woman called Colletta, and stole all her money."

"I know Colletta."

"She has accused a boy called Robert of the theft. I am told that Robert and your son are close friends. So I would like to ask your son a few questions."

"Did she see him steal the money? Was my son with him?"

"No, she didn't see who stole her money, but she thinks the boy Robert did it."

"Where were you last night?" the policeman asked Trevor.

"Robert came by in the afternoon, we hang around till about eight, then we went to the movies, then we left the movies around one and went home. We eh do nothing wrong."

Christine said, "that's true, his friend Robert came by that afternoon."

The policeman asked, "what movies were playing, what were the movies about?" Trevor had no problems answering these questions. Last night was the second time he and Robert had seen the three John Wayne movies.

"Who saw you at the movies?" A bunch of names rolled out of Trevor's mouth. The policeman knew that being at the movies was no alibi that the boys hadn't stolen the money. Colletta left her house at eleven-thirty and returned around two. So even if the boys had gone to the movies, there was plenty of time afterwards to steal the woman's money. After all, this was a five, ten-minute job. But the policeman didn't believe that the boys had stolen the money. This was done by seasoned criminals, not mere boys. He wouldn't even be surprised if, before the holidays were over, there was a string of such robberies. So the policeman was investigating Trevor halfheartedly. Besides, how could he conduct a proper interrogation with this never-before-seen beauty, staring at him, her eyes disapproving his every word?

"Sorry about interrupting your Christmas, Miss," said the policeman, and he strolled away, his body erect, his mind in turmoil.

As soon as the policeman was out of earshot, Christine turned to Trevor. "See what I've been telling you? That boy you love more than yourself, one of these days, will lead you straight to jail. Now tell me, did you, or did you not steal the woman's money?"

"No mom. We didn't steal nobody's money. That woman is a crazy liar, if she say we steal her money."

"Cut out this we business, because you didn't steal the money that doesn't mean your good-for-nothing friend didn't do it. You better stay clear of him, and tell him I don't want to see him near my house."

Colletta knew she wasn't a liar, and she was even surer of her sanity. She held fast to her suspicion. When she came across Felina, she looked the other way, and when it was Robert she stared at him long and hard. The last thing she did before she rested her head at night and the first thing she did when she got up in the morning was to kneel, her hand clutching her rosaries, and pray that God would curse whoever stole her money. Both she and God knew who the culprit was.

Heedless of the old woman's burning stares and unaware of her morning and evening curse ritual, Robert was enjoying the fruits of his hatred. He took out from his stolen bounty no more than fifteen dollars at a time. He held on to ten and gave Trevor the rest. They went more than once to every movie that played at Clarke and Gaiety. They stuffed themselves with *tablet*, shirley biscuits, chicken and beef rotis, dalpouri, chewing gum. They bought and smoke cigarettes by the pack, went to dances, and drank beer.

But they got more than food, movies, and cigarettes for their money. One mid-afternoon, two days after New Year, they were lazing out in an isolated corner of the Gardens when a girl of Robert's age came walking through. Robert drew the girl's attention and coaxed her into accepting one dollar for him and Trevor to see her breast, another to see her private parts, and another dollar to allow him to finger her. Then he unzipped his pants, let out his throbbing member, and offered the girl five dollars for him and his partner to have sex with her.

"I have seen bigger *lolo* than this," said the girl bravely. But then she pulled up her panties and ran away, turning her head back once to get a last view.

Robert wasn't dismayed. This whole scene was unplanned. He had just followed his urging on the spur of the moment. But his partial success with the girl made him realize that with his money he could get girls to do anything. So as the girl sped away, for five, ten dollars, he was picturing himself mounting girls all over the place.

Meanwhile, the rope that Felina had given Robert to hang himself was, unknown to him, beginning to tighten around his neck. She noticed that he wasn't gulping down his food as he usually did, nor complaining that she was giving his brother more food than him; nor was he attempting to steal food from his brother. On some days he didn't even show up for lunch. She also noticed that Ralph's appetite wasn't much better than his brother's.

Felina would get up in the small hours of the morning and search Robert's pockets for any sign of money. She never found any. Upon returning home, Robert always made sure of emptying his pockets of any left over money which he either gave Trevor for safe keeping or he hid in a cultivar hedge, not too for from home.

On the second day of the new year Felina pulled Ralph aside. "Ralph, don't lie to me. Have you seen Robert spending money?"

Ralph glanced at his mother, a glance that said that he would rather be in any other time than this moment, and in any other place than in his mother's presence. Then, focusing his eyes strictly on the hole for the missing button on his mother's bodice, he said, "no mom," in a voice that was just firm enough to be believable.

By now Robert had learned his lesson. He had learned that rather than making an enemy of Ralph, it paid to dull Ralph's tongue against him by tolerating him a little, letting Ralph hang around him and Trevor a bit. And during this season of goodwill and giving, he had made a point of sharing some of his bounty with his brother.

But Felina had become like a hound with the scent of her quarry all in her nostrils. She would not let up. "Boy, who you lying to? Do you think I was born yesterday? I'm asking you this, not because I don't already know the answer. I am just testing you. Now, for the last time, have you seen Robert spending money."

Equally determined, Ralph answered, "No mom. I don't see him spending no money."

"I see, so Robert has been spending some of that stolen money on you. You and him and that *douglah* boy that follows him every-where he goes went and steal the woman's money. Don't think I don't have eyes. I see how you does barely touch your food. How could you, when you are busy eating the woman's money? Well, well, well. I never thought that was how it would end. You in jail. Now I always knew that that brother of yours was as worthless as his spineless snake of a father, and it was just a matter of time before he would end up in jail. But I never thought you would follow in his footsteps. Well, I was wrong. Tomorrow I will go down to the police station and give them the whole story. You and your vagabond brother are going to rot in jail."

There were limits to which Ralph's tongued could be dulled. He wasn't about to rot in jail on account of a few matinees, a tablet here, a juicy there, a chicken and roti every once in a while.

"Mom, he and Trevor does spend money. But he say he find the money by the market a few days before Christmas. He say he don't steal no money."

"Your brother lie, he didn't find no money. He stole the woman's money. And since when are you in the habit of lying for your brother. I have a good mind to whip your behind. Now, listen. Your brother must have hid that money somewhere. I want you to keep an eye on him. Follow him, and watch where he does go get money."

Ralph wasn't going to jail for anybody. He obeyed his mother zealously. Four days into the new year, he followed Robert on a late Sunday afternoon to the burnt house, and there, behind the cover of bushes, he saw Robert pull out the milk tin, take out some money, look sideways in both directions, then slip the milk tin back under the bush. Ralph stayed hidden for ten minutes after Robert was gone. Then he crept to where he had seen his brother slide the milk tin. He opened the tin and saw more money than he had ever seen before. He left the tin of money there, and went and got his mother.

That night with the tin of money secure under her bed, Felina waited for morning. Earlier, under the threat of jail, she had made Ralph swore to silence. She knew exactly what she would do. Tonight she would say or do nothing to scare the boy. But in the early morning, while the fruits of his evil were still wearing off, she would get the police. They would apprehend him in bed. The father had gone unpunished for his misdeed, but if she had any say in the matter, the son would pay for his.

Just as she promised herself, at seven o'clock in the morning Felina returned home flanked by two policemen.

This was the fifth day of the New Year. The Savior was born and well on His way to Calvary. The Christmas carols extinguished. Empty rum, wine, beer and juicy bottles greeted the eye that peered into cupboards and cabinets hoping that the party was not yet over. Men dug into their pockets, looking for the hole through which their money had fallen out. Expatriates were beginning to pack; they had overstayed their welcome. Suddenly, the morning sun's glare was harsh and unforgiving.

Eyes followed Felina and the two policemen as they made their way to Felina's house. No one needed to be told. The accusing, vindictive voice of Colletta had been heard throughout the Conway, throughout the festive season. So the neighborhood watched with eyes beginning to sober up. They were thinking that if someone had told them that it was Felina's boy that had done it, they would never have believed it. But Colletta had told them so, yet they hadn't believed.

Ten minutes after the neighborhood's eyes followed Felina and the policemen into the house, they watched the policemen drag a handcuffed, struggling Robert-in-denial down the walk path away from the Conway.

It was one thing to savagely beat your son, or report him to the police, but it was another to watch the police drag him to jail. At the sight of the policemen taking Robert away, a pang of guilt, mixed with anger and fear struck Felina. Her first impulse was to run up to the policemen and beg for her son's release. But this impulse was soon followed by an overpowering need to cover up her feelings and to fight, to resist, this moment of weakness. So instead Felina screamed, "take him away. Take the *salòp* away. I have no child called Robert. Take the *Bouwo* away. "

The neighbors wondered, as they had many times before, how could a mother so hate a child?

Two hours later that morning the same two policemen came for Trevor. Christine was still in bed when she heard the knock. She asked herself, "what would somebody want at this hour of the night?" She had come in at four-thirty this morning. Her night was still lingering.

Trevor answered the knock, and immediately he knew this was it. His heart came to a halt, his mouth suddenly tasted bitter, and his color drained. The pair of eyes that looked into those of the policemen was that of a trapped animal that knew there was no escape. But he couldn't truthfully say he was surprised, for he had been half expecting the unexpected. His fears had come to be. He had let Robert do it to him again.

Hearing strange voices, Christine brought her night to an end, and came to the door. She was still in her night dress. The policemen's eyes rose above Trevor to take in the woman that appeared before them like an angel in a dream, her night dress revealing more than if she were stark naked. This picture would occupy their memories for a long time to come.

The sight of policemen at her doorsteps, and her son that smelled of fear, set Christine's heart racing. She completely forgot that she was in her night gown.

"What do you all want, this time? Hasn't he told you that he didn't do it? Don't you all have other things to do than coming here so early in the morning to harass my son? Why don't you go look for, what's his name, Robert? If anyone did anything, it will be that wharf-rat."

Looking at the angry woman in nightie, revealing perfection, the policemen had to fight hard to suppress the smiles that threatened to surface.

"Miss, we have already apprehended the boy Robert. We have undeniable proof that he stole Colletta's money. In fact we found the money, at least what is left of it. Your son, we understand was an accomplice to the theft, so we need to take him down for further questioning."

They took Trevor away. Unlike Robert, he went along meekly. His trapped, resigned eyes glued to the walk path. He heard his mother say, "Trevor, don't worry. As soon as I get dress I will be right down to straighten out all this nonsense." And as he walked between the two policemen, he was thinking that he couldn't remember his mother ever showing so much concern for his welfare.

The news traveled fast. But only Colletta's neighbors heard the truth. Outside of the Conway, the story was that it was two ten-year-olds who had stolen the old woman's money, but they were part of a theft ring that stretched from Vieux Fort to Castries.

Several other thefts had been committed the night of Christmas Eve. The police were looking for the ring leaders. People all over Castries locked their doors tight and secure as soon as dusk fell; children were warned not to tarry on the streets; cutlasses and hatchets were kept handy. On Monday, the banks' saving deposits increased by twenty-five percent.

The police flogged and locked up Robert and Trevor. Christine arrived soon after. She pleaded with the policemen. "Please let my son go. This is a mistake. My son doesn't have it in his heart to steal anyone's money."

Graced by such beauty, the policemen listened patiently to Christine. "Sorry," they said, "this is a matter for the police chief and the magistrate to decide."

In detention, still sobbing from his leather-belt flogging, Trevor was castigating Robert. "See what I was telling you. See. See. See where you put me, in your fucking ass. Why do I listen to you? It's always, always the same. You, asshole, said we eh go go to jail, we under age, what do you call this, heaven?"

"Man, shut your ass and leave me alone. This is just detention. We eh go see no jail time. I tired of explaining to you. Shut your ass, and leave me alone." Trevor sobbed some more and vowed never to follow his shadow again.

Christine left the police station, angry and full of dread. As soon as she got home, she took a shot of whiskey and went at Mrs. Stephen to make a phone call. Mr. Norman Blanchard, the headmaster of the St. Mary's College, answered her call.

"Christine, what the hell you calling me here for? Haven't I told you never to call me here."

"Trevor is in jail. You have to get him out."

"What did he do?"

"The police have him mixed up in some robbery, but I'm sure Trevor doesn't have it in his heart to rob anybody. It is some wharf-rat he limes with who stole the money, not my Trevor."

"Christine, you need to pay more attention to the boy, you

need to stop letting him run around in bad company."

"Don't tell me how to run my life. Are you going to get him out or not?"

"Christine, I am not the law. This is a matter for the law to take care of."

"Aren't you good friends with the police chief and the magistrate? For all I know, you all fucking the same *jabals*, concubines. Besides, I'm not talking about just any boy. In case you have forgotten, he is your son too."

"I don't want to get involved with that. If he didn't do it, then they will let him go."

"Bullshit! You got involved when you fucked me. Are you going to get him out or not?"

"Christine, .."

"Well, your wife will know who's the boy's father. Then we'll know whether or not you are involved."

"Alright, alright, I'll see what I can do. But you need to maintain better control over him."

The headmaster called the police chief. The police chief said that since the boys were under age they wouldn't go to jail, but he was of a mind to see that they were sent to Massade, the boy's correctional institution.

The headmaster pleaded, "I'm a good friend of Trevor's mother. This is the first time the boy has gotten into trouble with the law. Please let him go. I will owe you one."

"So you fucking his mother?"

"No, nothing like that. She is just a good friend of the family."

"I bet, a good friend indeed."

"Well, tell you what, I will let the boys go if they replace the money they spent, but I will keep them in jail for two more days to teach them a lesson, and next time you should be more careful where you shit."

On Monday, the headmaster paid whatever money Robert

and Trevor had spent, and Tuesday morning Robert and Trevor stepped into the sunlight. "What did I tell you," said Robert. Didn't I tell you we eh go go to jail?"

Trevor didn't answer, but he silently vowed never again to follow his shadow.

8

Ten P.M. Monday, June 19, 1948. Justin Lamontagne had just gotten rid of his last client of the day, bringing another marathon day at his tailor-shop to a close. The client's suit was two weeks overdue and he had been fussing about having to leave for England in the morning without his suit. While he waited for Justin Lamontagne to iron the suit and put buttons on the jacket, he chain-smoked. But in the end he had left the tailor shop pleased that the suit he held in his hands was made by the best tailor on the island, a man who had learned his trade in England, the motherland. As Lamontagne locked his shop for the night, the satisfaction he felt when he had handed his client the finished suit, and his client's nervous belligerence had turned into smiles of gratitude and relief, lingered.

On the way home, while Lamontagne was thinking about the possibilities of expanding his tailor shop, a pair of pants completed save for hemming and ironing, slipped from a partition wall and fell over the ashtray containing the cigarette butts of the once belligerent customer. Unfortunately, some of the cigarette stubs weren't out completely. The garment caught fire, burning the cloth, and clothes patterns lying on the table. And with so much cloth and garments lying on the sewing machines and hanging all over the shop, the house was soon ablaze.

The gods of the land, seeing an opportunity to destroy Castries, their longtime nemesis, once and for all, sent a strong southeasterly wind that carried the fire from the tailor shop at the corner of Chisel and Brazil Street to neighboring buildings, and then from building to building. In a moment Castries was in flames.

People awoke to the heat and smell and choking smoke of fire. Taken by surprise, grown men, realizing that the heat they were feeling was hotter than the heat of their passion, jumped out of their love nests and rushed naked unto the streets. Bewildered women ran out of their houses screaming and clutching sleeping children.

When people caught on to the fire, they formed lines to haul buckets of water from stand-pipes to the burning buildings, but they soon realized that their efforts were as futile as trying to drain the Caribbean Sea with buckets. Besides, the heat was so intense that getting close enough to throw water over the fire was next to impossible. Propelled by the wings of the gods, the fire burned out of control. Most people were forced to give up on saving their worldly possessions and settle for saving just their lives and those of their neighbors.

The ill-equipped Castries fire brigade was late in respond-ing to the fire and their timid efforts weren't much more effective than those of the people hauling buckets of water. The fire burned all night.

Seventeen-year-old Felina, living with her aunt since the death of her mother five years before, was dreaming. In her dream she was being buried, buried under mountains of coal, and it was dark. The coals suddenly caught fire and it got hot. Smoke was everywhere, and she was choking; she was gasping for air, gasp-ing and coughing. Then her world started to shake, as if an earth-quake was in progress. Horrified, remembering a similar sensation eleven years ago on the night of the landslides, she awoke from her dream to find her aunt shaking her vigorously, and screaming, "get up, get up, the house is on fire. Castries is burning."

Eight months and two weeks pregnant, Felina rose sluggishly from the bed as she gasped for air in the room that was already filled with smoke and which was about to go up in flames. Not waiting for Felina to fully gain consciousness, the aunt grabbed her around the shoulders and half-dragged, half-walked her out of the house and onto the pavement. No sooner had she sat Felina on the sidewalk, Felina's water broke. All around was chaos: people running out of houses, screaming; some hurriedly grabbing furniture and other valuables from the jaws of the fire; panicky mothers calling out to children. Luckily, a police jeep circling the city, keeping an eye on looters and other opportunists, was passing on Grass Street, within shouting distance of where Felina was seated on Coral Street. The police heeded the plaintive call of Felina's aunt and took the prostrate, expectant mother to Victoria Hospital, situated on a hill overlooking the Caribbean Sea, a good distance from the raging fire.

Felina was the first victim of the fire brought to the hospital, so unlike the other victims to come, she received the full and immediate attention of the hospital staff. For that Felina needed to be thankful, because no sooner had the hospital staff laid her on the maternity bed, the baby started making its way into the world.

"Push, push, you are almost there. That's it. That's it," said the doctor. A nurse wiped beads of sweat forming on Felina's forehead.

"You are almost there. There it comes, there it comes. One last push, one last push."

A baby boy emerged with his umbilical cord wrapped around his neck. He was pale and blue. The doctor quickly uncoiled the cord from the baby's neck, tied and cut the cord, forced the baby's mouth open and for brief, intermittent periods applied an oxygen mask to the baby's face until he coughed and started breathing on his own. The baby was lucky. If he had been born just a few minutes later, he would have been stillborn. The nurses kept him under close observation throughout the night. Miraculously, by the early morning hours the baby had regained his color and was like any other newborn.

It turned out that the baby's biggest problem wasn't the condition of his birth but his mother. What the umbilical cord wrapped around the baby's neck had failed to do, his mother was threatening to do. When, after the baby had gained normalcy, one of the nurses had placed him on Felina's stomach, she made no effort to touch her baby, neither did she once glance at him. Worse, she refused to breast-feed him. The nurse had to take the crying baby away and bottle-feed him.

It wasn't always so. Unlike many unwed teenage mothers, when Felina had found out that she was pregnant, she had been overjoyed. She was carrying a piece of the man she loved. Besides, having (by the age of five) lost her father and siblings to the great landslide of 1938 and (by the age of twelve) her mother to coaldust, she was more anxious than most to start her own family. In her happiness and naivete, Felina had no doubt that Benoit, her nineteen-year-old boyfriend, her life, her god, would be just as elated over the news. She had no way of knowing that at nineteen the last thing Benoit, the seventh of nine children, wanted was raising a child. Benoit was Felina's first and only boyfriend, her first love. She was yet to gain the distrustfulness, the sourness, that would have enabled her to see through her boyfriend, to see that he had been going along with the love-thing, the dreaming, the planning, just to get into her panties.

With a beaming smile, Felina had approached Benoit. "We are starting a family."

"What do you mean?" he asked. Felina's beaming smile had changed in midstream to disappointment as the primitive flight syndrome registered on Benoit's face, even before he had asked the question.

"I'm having a baby," she answered, her voice deflated.

"A baby! Are you sure?" Confused and shocked by his reaction, she volunteered no reply.

"Whose it is?" With this question her confusion turned into anger.

"What do you mean whose it is? Whose do you think?

"I don't know, but it can't be mine. Each time we did it, I made sure I pulled out before I came."

As these words were spoken, Felina's world, her future, her dreams and aspirations, had begun to crumble. Piercing through her confusion, the tears that were streaming down her face and her anger, was the realization that all the while she had been believing in an illusion. The pain she felt was more acute than that of losing her father and siblings on the night of the landslides or her mother on the night of the barking dogs. The shock of her boyfriend's words, the feeling of how could she have been so wrong, wouldn't allow Felina to plead her case then or ever. A voice deep in her psyche, a voice sounding older than her years, kept repeating: "it's happening again; it's happening again; again and again. First your father and your brothers and sisters, then your mother, and now this betrayal, this lie, this thing that never was. Love is death, loving is dying." The voice prevented Felina from begging, pleading, from forcing Benoit to see how much she loved him, from forcing him to see reason, if not passion.

Three years before, at the public standpipe, she had first met Benoit. Then he had taunted her, asking her name, telling her how short her hair was, and how small a bucket of water she was carrying. She had ignored him, as if he didn't exist, but she hadn't failed to notice the strong broad shoulders and muscular arms that carried away two buckets of water. Six months had passed before she begun acknowledging his presence and started to answer his questions, and another six months before she said, "yes," to his persistent question, "will you be friendly to me?" For the next eight months, though she had come to the conclusion that he was her prince, her future, the father of her children, tongue kissing was the most she had allowed him. But soon, convinced of her love for him and his love for her, she gradually let herself go.

At the beach, one Sunday afternoon, after swimming and frolicking in the water, they had sat on the bleached sand and, while watching the sun go down, they fell into their usual habit of discussing and dreaming about their future. For the hundredth time he told her about his apprenticeship at the furniture shop.

"In two or three more years I will definitely own my own shop and in next than no time I will be a big time furniture man-ufacturer, a big shot, employing tens of people, providing the whole island with furniture. Maybe I will even set up my own retail outlets which you, my darling, will manage."

She had believed him before and she believed him then. This fitted exactly with what she had daydreamed while watching her mother and the other charbonniers die a slow death under the hun-dredweight baskets of coal. Her dream was materializing. The promise she had made to herself ten years ago would be kept— the promise of never slaving for anyone like her mother had done. As the sun bordered the horizon, casting fiery-gold on the blue of the Caribbean, Benoit held her hands and led her under the sea-grape and sea-almond trees lining the beach. The sound future in wait, the quiet and cooling afternoon, and the soft, comforting whistling of the trees swaying gently in the calm Caribbean breeze gave Felina a profound sense of security and there, in the secrecy of the sea-almond and sea-grape foliage, she gave herself, for the first time, wholly to the man of her future, the man who would help her keep the promise she had made to herself.

After that afternoon on the beach, nothing could keep Felina away from her man. Her Aunt warned her. "I know that I'm not your mother, but take my advice, girl. Men are like snakes; they ain't too particular who they bite. They so caring and loving when they hunting you, but after they get you they run away as swift as mongoose. They taste like honey in your mouth, but like bile in your throat. You have suffered and lost enough. I don't want to see you hurt no more. Beware of that boy, the boy you can't get enough of."

She had paid her Aunt no mind. "This woman is old," she told herself. "She doesn't know what she is talking about. That's if she has ever had a man."

After a year of bliss, of passion, of plans and dreams, the words, "whose it is . . ., it can't be mine . . ." was too much for Felina to bear. The echo of the words of betrayal ringing in her ears mingled with the voice that sounded older than her years—the voice that kept repeating: "it's happening again, it's happening again, again and again; first your father and your brothers and sisters, then your mother, and now this betrayal, this lie, this thing that never was; love is death, loving is dying"—she ran oblivious of where she was going, and her run congealed into a hatred. A hatred stronger than her hatred of God for allowing her mother to die in a pool of blood on the night of the barking dogs. Her hatred of her boyfriend grew as strong as her love once was. It was as if she had transferred her hatred of God to her boyfriend and multiplied that hatred tenfold. "Love is death, loving is dying," she found herself repeating like a mantra.

Three times she came looking for Benoit with a knife. The first two times three of Benoit's brothers wrestled her to the ground and took the knife away. The third time she didn't find Benoit. He had run away to live with his father's relatives in Millet. With her boyfriend gone, Felina turned her hatred to her unborn child.

Three months pregnant, she paid a visit to Ms. Elvie, a Pavee woman known to have a bush-potion for every condition including throwing away children. Ms. Elvie looked at the three-month, pregnant girl, asking with a quiet determination for a potion to throw away her child, and decided that this strong, coal-black girl was more than fit to have her baby. So instead of a throw-away-child potion she gave Felina a portion for headaches. Felina waited a whole month for the baby to start dissolving, but instead her belly continued to swell. "That Ms. Elvie is one quack!" she said aloud, and decided to get rid of her baby using her own methods. Twice she fell off her bed, but her only reward was a backache. The baby continued to grow. Finally, she resigned herself to the inevitable and thought of the many accidents that could happen to the baby after he or she was born. Felina was determined, one way or the other, to eradicate all traces of her boyfriend's betrayal. And so was Robert, a child conceived in love, born in the vengeance fire of the gods and the fire of his mother's hatred.

Felina awoke at dawn to the smell of smoke and the feel of her baby which one of the nurses had placed on her stomach during the early morning hours after the baby seemed fine. The hospital had been active all night treating burnt victims. Castries was still burning.

When people as far away from Castries as Vieux Fort opened their doors in the morning, the first thing they noticed was smoke billowing across the sky. A smoke-cloud hovered over the whole island. During the night, the night of the city's death by fire, the lighthouse at Vigie was redundant. The flames of Castries were visible miles away from shore.

At six in the morning the firefighting squad of the United States Airforce in Vieux Fort answered Castries's call for help. When they arrived in Castries later that morning, three-fifths of the city was already consumed. Headed by Sergeant Anthony Cummings, the army's firefighters fought a whole day against the fire. By early evening, when they had finally won the battle, four-fifths of the city had been reduced to coal and ashes. The wilderness of ashes, the smoldering coals, the burnt galvanized sheets and concrete foundations, and the dumbfounded and dejected look of the crowd that had gathered around the American firefighters as they packed away their fire fighting equipment gave Castries the look of Hiroshima after the bombing.

Looking into the crowd, Anthony Cummings eyes stayed transfixed on a sixteen-year-old girl. The girl's long hair was in disarray and sprinkled with ashes. Her face was grim and marked by traces of tear drops, and her dress was torn in places and blackened as if she had just come out of a coal mine. Strangely, the girl's dismal condition seemed to accentuate her beauty.

The gods of the land had not saved Christine, their own daughter, from their fire of vengeance. She was among the two-thousand and ninety-three people the fire had made homeless. The homeless daughter of the gods of the land returned and held the stare of the man whom it seemed God had sent to save what was left of the city.

In years to come Anthony Cummings would forget the grim face, the ash-sprinkled hair, and the dress that reminded him of a coal mine, but not the pair of lucent eyes that seemed to pronounce him a god. Every time that pair of eyes would penetrate his consciousness, an uneasiness would settle over him.

9

Christine, the child conceived in a crucible of love and passion in which the spirit of Africa joined with India, was no ordinary child. She was born with a love and knowledge of men. This coupled with her matchless beauty continued to baffle people long after she returned to the womb.

Christine had come out crying, as if she didn't want to be born. But as soon as her father, Leonce, had entered the maternity room and Christine's unfocused eyes had found the direction of his voice, her cry had given way to suckling sounds of contentment. At three months, it was her father, not the one she suckled, that Christine followed around with her eyes. She would be passive and indifferent all day, but as soon as her father made his entrance she brightened up and made gleeful sounds. Not much older than a year, Christine took a distinct pleasure in rolling over her father. But with her mother she was quiet and reserved. When Christine was about two years old, Leonce noticed that she concentrated her rolling on his crotch. At first, this predisposition of Christine hadn't alarmed Leonce. "She is so innocent," he said to himself, "she doesn't know what she is doing." But a year later, when Christine began to massage his crotch with some deliberation, causing a bulge, and he was more ashamed of himself than shocked at the dexterity of his daughter's fingers, he knew he had a special problem on his hands. From then on he kept Christine's hands in check and he did his best to make sure that she didn't roll or rub her body on the place she most favored.

Leonce's real troubles began when Christine entered her teens, when her body was entering womanhood. On her way outside to shower out of a drum of collected rain water, Christine would stretch languidly in her father's full view, and she would give him that smile that he had come to know so well, and it would take all of his will power to keep his mind off the jungle of grass sprouting out on the sides of her flimsy panties, and off her breasts that stood as pointed and shapely as the gods of the land—breasts begging to be touched, to be suckled. Christine's vanishing nakedness would leave Leonce weak and sweating, but his torture continued. The moan of his daughter as the icy rainwater kissed her tender skin sounded like a woman in the depth of her love throes.

During each encounter Leonce tried to keep a poker face, but Christine was born with a knowledge of men that was as natural as her suckling instinct. She knew and enjoyed the confused desire of her father. She never planned to tempt him, she had never given the matter much thought. It just felt good, tingling, to smile and languor almost naked in front of her father, and shower in the desire his eyes emitted. It was no different from her ravishing a julee mango. Both were delicious.

Soon Leonce started timing his daughter's baths so he would be no where near when she appeared like a virgin to the altar. But the small, two-bedroom house made his daughter difficult to avoid.

Leonce need not have been so hard on himself. He wasn't the only one Christine bewitched. Her spell had been evident since preschool. Little boys somehow felt bigger than themselves when they were with Christine, their beautiful classmate. If the boys were a little older, they would have expressed it as: "Christine makes me feel like a man." But all they knew then was that to be with Christine was to feel special, to feel privileged. A smile, an eye flutter, a pursed lip, was to the little boys the equivalent of sex. Surrounded by so much male attention, Christine grew even more beautiful. And as she graduated from one class to the next it was always: "Christine, the beautiful girl in the class," and the rest of the girls.

The girls at school kept their distance from Christine. They were jealous of all the male attention she received and accepted so graciously, the "nice hair" reaching to her buttocks, the copper-brown skin that was as smooth and soft as velvet, and the face, a lesson in symmetrical perfection, that glowed with femininity and a born knowledge of men.

Christine didn't mind the girls' predisposition towards her at all. From birth she had preferred the company of men. Even before she began tormenting her father with her bathing rituals the neighborhood boys were always finding some excuse—they came to pick up a cricket ball, to ask if so and so lived there, to ask about a lost black cat—to drop by the house in the hope of seeing and speaking to Christine. She never failed to show her face. A smile from her was more than enough reward for the boys' deceit. A gang of boys accompanied her on her way home from school, each boy trying to get as close to Christine as possible, each jostling for the privilege of carrying her books. In Christine's company, each boy tried to out do the other. The taunts became meaner, the jokes bolder, the cricket or soccer game took on greater meaning, each boy playing his best, his fanciest. Soccer or cricket was no more a team sport. It was a game of individuals, each competing against the other, notwithstanding that the other was on the same team. As if such displays weren't enough, the boys showered her with candies, mangoes, oranges. The other girls stood sullenly on the side, and watched the movie unfold.

By the time Christine turned sixteen, three years since she started tormenting her father, when her girlish smile had turned coquettish, when curvature was added to her already perfect body, when sway and poise were added to her walk, and when her breast had developed and taken after the image of the gods of the land, she was more woman than most women could ever hope to be. Without even trying she had achieved a femininity that took most women years of effort to achieve. Old people dug in their memories to find someone more beautiful or as beautiful as Christine, but they came up with no one. Some shook their heads and wondered, how many hearts will that child break?

No matter what previous image of the perfect woman that a man held, after laying eyes on Christine his image of the perfect woman became Christine. Upon passing Christine, married women subconsciously clutched their men more tightly, single women looked up with envy, men suspended whatever they were doing and paid rapt attention. In the night, while making love to their wives or girlfriends, many men imagined that it was Christine they were entering.

The old people, accustomed to tracing lineage and determining from which ancestor so and so got their height, their "nice" hair, their light skin, their big nose, their big behinds, wondered from where the girl had gotten her looks. It couldn't be from her parents, because by any standard the father was ugly, and, save for "nice" hair and fair skin, the mother was so-so.

To find out from whom Christine got her looks, these old people would have had to go back two thousand years, when the gods of the land had sent the Caribs to invade the land and kill and drive away the Arawaks. Towards the end of the battle, the Carib chief caught a glimpse of the most beautiful creature he had ever laid eyes on fleeing with her companion toward the beach. The Carib chief didn't know it then, but the companion was the Arawak chief and the beautiful creature was his wife, Candence. The Caribs had already won the battle for the island and the chief was exhausted, so ordinarily he would have let the two fleeing shadows be. But the glimpse of beauty that had caught his eyes led him to launch the arrow that would claim the life of the Arawak chief. Stupefied with anguish and fright, Candence fell prostrate over her dead husband. But she need not have feared for herself. The following day the Carib chief proclaimed Candence his wife. Her beauty had caused the death of her husband, but had saved her from the arrow of her future husband.

Nearly seventeen hundred years later, in the era of the revenge of the gods on the Caribs for allowing the French to move the capital from Soufrière to Castries, Laborie, a French sugar plantation owner operating in the Mabouya Valley, raped a descendent of Candence. Since the boy-child that resulted from the encounter came out even whiter than Laborie himself, he accepted his son, named him Laborie Jr. and passed him as white.

Twenty-five years after the night of the rape and three years after the death of Laborie Sr., when Laborie Jr. had inherited his father's plantation, Laborie Jr. was attending an auction of slaves fresh from Africa. Save for entertainment he had no specific reason for attending the auction. His sugarcane plantation was well stocked with slaves of both sexes. He even had an adequate supply of breeder slaves. Laborie Jr. was looking on the auction with slight interest when this woman was brought to the auction block. This wasn't the first woman sold at the auction that day and this one in leg chains and tattered clothes that left her full, pointed breast exposed, was dressed no different from the other women. But her haughty, queenly gaze and sensuous beauty stirred the loins of every man present. Each man felt like a horse rider who, having just caught a magnificent horse, was anticipating the joy of breaking the horse and the thrill of sailing the wind. The auction went into a frenzy, each man desperately needing to win the prize. As the bid increased beyond reason, the auction became a crucible of passion. One by one the men melted away, until only the man that most passionately desired the woman remained standing. That man was Laborie Jr. He had won his slave at a cost tenfold the market price of a healthy female. No one had any memory of a slave selling so high above the market rate. Laborie Jr. took his slave home where she served his wife during the day and serviced him during the night. Christine's father was a descendent of the first child that Laborie Junior's prized female slave bore him.

Still, even without such an intimate knowledge of history, if, instead of the gods of Europe, the people were believers of the gods of the land, they might have guessed that Christine was a child of the gods, and, notwithstanding the means and ways, they would have known it was the gods that had imbued her with such beauty. Or, if instead of paying so much homage to the beaches, which spoke of greed, annihilation and slavery, the people had paid more respect to the gods of the land which once provided them with refuge from enslavement and now from touristic contamination, the people would have noticed that Christine had been fashioned after the very image and beauty of the gods.

So without a memory that extended way back into the past and having paid so little homage to the gods of the land, the people were left to wonder, long after Christine entered her grave, from where and from whom she had inherited her beauty.

To the dismay of the gods of the land, it didn't take long for Castries to resurrect from its fiery grave. With over four hundred thousand dollars in fire relief funds and a million-pound grant from the government of the Windward Islands, Castries entered a construction boom. There was work for every bum, every wharf-rat. Professional drunks who couldn't remember when last they held a job found employment. People flocked to Castries from every cranny of the island. They came from Augier, Getrine, Fond Coolie, La Croix Maingot, Trou Bananes, Mahaut, Fond St. Jacques, La Retraite, Fond d' Asou, Bois d' Orange, Jacmel, Esperance, Dugard, La Fargue, Londonderry, Mamiku, La Ressource, everywhere. No one could remember when last things were so nice. Some people couldn't help thinking that someone would do the island a big favor if ever so often, ten years maybe, that someone would burn down Castries. This vexed the gods of the land exceedingly. Here they were, thinking they had imposed a severe punishment on Castries, yet it seemed they had done Castries a favor.

If the people were aware of the sentiments of the gods of the land, they didn't show it. On the contrary, by the time Carnival came around, two years after the cities death by fire, people were in a festive mood. They were ready to celebrate, to jump-up and dance, to shake the ashes of the fire off their clothes and shoes, to put all that death business behind their backs, and to begin life anew. After all, their city was no more that clustered, dirty, coaling station. It was now a modern city of boulevards, of suburbs, a city that could stand up proudly among other West Indian cities, a city fit for a capital. The gods of the land fumed.

Carnival came, and never before had the people partied so hard. The streets of Castries flowed with rum, whiskey, and bacchanal. Never before had calypso sounded so good, nor steel pan so sweet. The people danced and gyrated all day, all night, for three days. The streets of Castries were so jam-packed with people that it seemed like they could hold not one more reveller.

All the parade bands chose a city's death by fire as their theme. Their costumes were fiery red, and were designed to look as if they were ablaze. All the color shades of fire were represented, the costume of each band displaying a different shade. From the air Castries appeared like a long, gyrating inferno. The people had made a mockery of the revenge of the gods of the land.

Leading the parade, the gyrating inferno, was Christine, the child of the gods, the year's Carnival Queen.

Six months before Carnival, as soon as Christine had hinted about entering the Carnival Queen contest the word had carried fast. So much so that she had no need to go looking for sponsors. Within days they—Barclays Bank, J.Q. Charles, M&C, and others—had come knocking. The business sector had known what everyone who had laid eyes on Christine knew: a bird of such rare beauty would wear the crown. Christine had chosen Barclays Bank as her sponsor.

Although Christine was used to being the one all eyes focused on, especially those of men, she had been a bit flustered with all the fussing and pampering she received during the designing and making of her garments and during preparation for appearances. But through out the Carnival Queen competition, as soon as she walked on stage in swimsuit, and evening wear, all her bewilderment vanished. Every time she appeared on stage, the audience gasped. Each time was like the first time. The people knew they were witnessing beauty, elegance, and poise never before seen. Yet she is so young, they all thought.

Christine strolled on stage, smiling like a benevolent queen upon her subjects, bringing her audience to an exquisite ecstasy, each of her poses fit for immortality. She became one with the gods of the land. This is heaven, she thought. This is my kingdom, and these are my subjects.

What no one doubted was realized. Christine was crowned queen. To the people, there was no close second. She could win any beauty pageant in the world, they thought. She should have entered the Trinidad Carnival Queen contest. No one would stand a chance against her. No one.

In this carnival, the carnival celebrating the rebirth of Castries, the carnival like none other, before or after, the carnival that thwarted the will of the gods, Christine, the child of the gods, led her subjects, her kingdom, the carnival parade, the gyrating inferno. Flanked by her runners-up, she sat on a makeshift throne on top of the wooden hood of a passenger truck. She was dressed in a sparkling, silvery gown. Her exquisite, jeweled, golden crown blazed in the afternoon heat. She waved to the gyrating inferno, her subjects. She was caught in a dream world, in a whirlpool of ecstasy, she was doing what came naturally, what she was born to do. She swayed to the beat of calypso, and the rhythm of steel drums. She sipped rum and coke; she floated, floated over her kingdom. Never before had the people witnessed a carnival so thrilling. Never before had they a Carnival Queen so fit to be queen, a Carnival Queen that so graced the throne.

Although the child of the gods was born with a love and knowledge of men, she was yet to know men. But this carnival of fire, of passion, was soon to change that.

On the night of the first day of carnival, the Carnival Committee held a party for the Calypso King and Carnival Queen contestants and all the carnival parade organizers. As Carnival Queen, Christine was the toast of the party. Everyone wanted to congratulate her. "Oh how beautiful she looked! There has never been a Carnival Queen as graceful and beautiful as she. She has brought great honor to this year's carnival." Every man at the party was thinking, oh, how I would like to spend the night with her, the perfect dish after a day of jumping up!

Sipping rum and coke, calypso music vibrating through her sensuous body, Christine glowed under all the adulation. She talked, smiled, and enchanted everyone, making every man feel special, but gracefully averting their subtle and not so subtle advances.

Among the men at the party, none paid Christine as much attention as Norman Blanchard, headmaster of St. Mary's College, and one of the judges of the Carnival Queen competition. Throughout the Calypso King and Queen competition, Norman Blanchard had stayed close to Christine, admiring her poise, her grace, her unrivaled beauty. As the party progressed, he kept a close eye on Christine, watching her eyes dance, watching her move effortlessly through the crowd, dazzling everyone. Each time a man came up to Christine, a pang of fear invaded his body. It was like he and Christine were long time lovers, and every man at the party was trying to take his lover away from him. Christine was his rose, his well-spring, his delicacy. He danced with Christine as often as the other men at the party allowed him. He silently cursed each time someone came talking to him, pulling him away from his passion, creating opportunities for other men to get to his lover. He was even more alarmed when, as he saw it, another man stole a dance with Christine, causing him to force down another drink to calm his jealousy.

Two days before, he had made sure to offer Christine a ride to the party, and he would make sure she left with him. He wasn't taking any chances. He had to close off all opportunities of another man taking his Christine away from him. But his plans for the night went further than that. In his pocket were keys to the home of an elderly British couple who were spending time in England. Their home was only five houses down the road from the party. The couple had left the house in the care of their neighbor, a good friend of the headmaster. Yesterday the headmaster had secured the keys from his friend. He was prepared.

Christine, for her part, had noticed the headmaster's eyes following her around. Since she entered the Carnival Queen contest, in every direction she turned he seemed to be there, with a gleam in his eyes. The same gleam she had noticed in her father's eyes when his eyes made contact with her naked body, on her way to her icy, rainwater bath. As was the case with her father, the craze, the desire in the headmaster's eyes amused, tingled her, made her feel more a woman. At the party their eyes met often, her eyes dancing, sparkling like the stars, and his piercing, burning with a jealous passion. She danced with him, again and again. Each time she could feel his bulge rubbing against her belly as they gyrated to the beat of calypso. She smiled then, liking the feel of his manhood, teasing him, driving him to the point of being willing to kill for her. And the part that amused her most was the jealous rage that spread over his face when she went dancing with someone else.

By two A.M., the headmaster could no longer bear the torture. Better quit while I'm ahead. Better leave now before I lose her, the headmaster was thinking. Too many sharks in the water.

So at two, though the party was still going strong, Christine and the headmaster took their leave. As they bade their goodbyes, all the men looked upon the headmaster with envy. They realized that it could just as well have been them walking out with the Carnival Queen. So she was there for the taking, they thought. If they had known, they wouldn't have let her slip through their grasps. The single men, those in their twenties, wondered what was she doing with that married man, fifteen, twenty years older than herself. He could be her father, for Christ's sake. Those who had come to the party with their girlfriends or their wives wished they had left them at home. Only the women at the party were happy to see Christine go. The spotlight could now shine on them.

With all the night's adulation and praise, calypso music playing sweet melodies in her ear, rum and coke telling funny jokes in her head, and a man old enough to be her father treating her as a princess, a queen, and hot with desire for her, Christine was enjoying the lightness of being. She stepped out of the party, the headmaster comfortably close. She looked up at the stars and then started to laugh. All the stars were shining on her, transforming her into the brightest of stars. A star fell from the sky, and she let go another happy laugh that filled the night; or so thought the headmaster. I have just displaced a star, thought Christine. The night's breeze massaged her face, intensifying her intoxication.

So light was Christine that when the car came to a stop next to a house several houses down the road from the party they had just left, and the headmaster mumbled, "let us go in for a while," Christine didn't raise one thread of objection. They entered the house, the headmaster's arms wrapped around her waist, like two people who have been a couple for years. It had been a perfect carnival, it had been a perfect night, and the child of the gods was as ripe for love as a graham mango too ripe to stay hanging on the tree.

Christine's glow of the moment, her lightness of being, turned into love, love for the headmaster, a man who could be her father.

She nestled in his arms, calypso playing soft melodies in her ear, rum and coke whispering romantic tales, the headmaster's kisses, his touch, his murmurs of passion replaced the massaging night breeze, transporting her to new worlds. Whatever little restraint she had left dissolved. She gave herself wholly to him. She twisted and moaned. He unclothed her slowly, relishing the moment, giving his eyes utmost pleasure, not fully believing he had captured such a precious prize. He entered her. And the child who was born with a love and knowledge of men, but who had yet to know men, moved as if she had made love hundreds of times before. She anticipated his every move, she moved in perfect rhythm with him. The headmaster was buried in a depth-less cloud, and in that cloud he left a piece of himself.

Since that first night, the night of the party, the night of calypso, and rum and coke, the night the child of the gods got to know men, they continued under the cover of night to make love at the British couple's house until the couple returned from England, and at the headmaster's house when his wife and kids were out visiting his wife's parents in Dennery. When their need for each other was too great for containment and no love nest offered itself, they made love on the beach, in the evening, under the arms of sea-almond and sea-grape trees.

Then Christine broke the news to the headmaster—she was pregnant—and the news turned the headmaster's love into avoidance. If his wife, the mother of his five children, found out about this affair, this illegitimacy, this would be the end of his fifteen-year marriage. So he told Christine he couldn't see her anymore and she must never tell anyone that the child was his. But she mustn't worry; he would buy her a house and help support the child.

The words of the headmaster turned Christine's love into despair. His words were daggers twisting in her heart. Although she was born with a knowledge of men, this betrayal, this treachery, was one side of men of which she was ignorant. She found out what Felina had found out some time ago. She was heart bro-

ken. "You bastard, what you take me for, a *jamet*? You use me
and now you want to discard me like a dirty rag. You are no man.
You are a coward, a traitor. Is that what you teach your students—
deceit and cowardice? Take your house and shove it up your ass.
Go to hell."

Soon after that outburst Christine entered a deep depression.
For almost three weeks, despite the constant scolding of her mother,
she went nowhere and ate little. She lost fifteen pounds and turned
into the shadow of the stunningly beautiful queen that once graced
the carnival throne and mesmerized a nation. On the Thursday morning of the third week of her depression, she fainted and fell. The doctors at Victory Hospital kept her five days under observation.

It was during Christine's stay at the hospital that her parents
found out she was pregnant.

Both parents were furious. They became even more furious
when Christine refused to say who the father was. "None of you
all business," she kept repeating.

Leonce turned on his wife. "It is this carnival business that
has turned her into a whore. When I said that no daughter of mine
is going up for Carnival Queen, is going to parade her body like
a whore in front of the whole world, you refused to back me up.
Instead you fussed, and said that this was a great opportunity, this
was good exposure for her, one never knows how far winning
Carnival Queen will take one. You said that the girl has so many
sponsors. After she wins she will have no problem getting an office
job. She got exposure all right, she got jobs all right."

Julita, guilty of the same indiscretion as her daughter eighteen years ago, never responded to her husband's bantering. But
with her Christine found no peace. Morning, noon and night Julita
lambasted her daughter.

"A little Carnival Queen you win and you think that gave
you license to open your legs to any man that whistles. I didn't
raise any daughter to be a whore. And what is worse, you don't
even know who the father is. Who you expect is going to feed

your child? I bet you didn't think of that when you were lying down all over the place. Oh, you think beauty is all? You think a pretty face is security against anything. Well, my daughter, I have news for you. I have a mind to kick you out of my house, and let me see how far your pretty face will take you. You think most men are like your father. Ha! Ha! Ha! Well, let me tell you. Men are like bees. When the flower is blooming they swarm you and suck all your honey, but as soon as your honey drys up and your flower begins to fade they move on to flowers in full bloom."

Morning, noon and night Christine had to listen to such castigations. Once she got so fed up that she said to her mother, "if I'm a whore you are just as big a whore, because although you were promised to another you interfered with my father. Is you who taught me. I followed in your footsteps. And stop talking about this shack as your house. You are renting this shack, remember. This isn't your house."

When Christine said this, Julita cried and didn't say a word to her daughter for a whole week. But it seemed like Julita had used the week to gather up her ammunition, because at the end of the week when she started to chastise Christine again, her attacks were more vehement.

"Who would have thought that the daughter I gave up my whole world for would one day call me a whore? The daughter I conceived in pain and suffering. I loved your father with my whole heart, and I will love him till I die. I did not go sleeping around, opening my legs for every man that winked my way. And I knew who my child's father was, and that father is the one who is putting food on this table, and who has provided a roof over your head. A shack it may be, but a roof nonetheless. I have loved one man, and for the rest of my life I will love one man.

"You say you are like me. But nothing can be further from the truth. I knew who my child's father was, and when I was with child I left my parent's house and joined my child's father, your father. I don't see you moving in with your child's father. How could you, when you don't even know who the father is? You were a child conceived in love, the love of your father and mine. You weren't conceived in bacchanal as is that fatherless child growing in your belly. No. You have not followed in my footsteps, you have followed the life of the streets."

Four months into her pregnancy, Christine had had enough. She swallowed her pride and went to see the headmaster. Yes, she would take the house, and, yes, she would not make trouble for him. She would not tell anyone he was the father, but in addition to the house he would have to give her money every month to support his child. The headmaster agreed. So a month later, Christine moved into a two-bedroom house in the Conway.

The following day Mrs. Stephen came by to find out who her pregnant neighbor was. She took immediate pity on the beautiful, pregnant girl that was too young to be living alone, more so pregnant. This would be one of many visits Mrs. Stephen would make to the home of her beautiful neighbor. In fact, as the months passed, she would become her neighbor's big sister.

Less than three years after the city's death by fire the child of the gods gave birth to a son whom she named Trevor. Despite the circumstances surrounding her pregnancy and the birth of her son, unlike Felina, she didn't form a hatred for her betrayed love, neither did she harbor a misplaced hatred for her son. Her experience with the headmaster had taught her never to fall in love with men, but she still loved men. After her child was born it didn't take long for her life to take off. She was still a celebrity, after all. Pregnant or not pregnant, children or no children, she was still the most beautiful woman in the land. Men flocked to her. No. She didn't hate her son, but she was too busy living to pay him much attention. So Mrs. Stephen became not only big sister to her neighbor, but mother and babysitter to her neighbor's son. No. Unlike Felina, Christine didn't hate her son, but, as fate would have it, the hatred of a son would produce just about the same result as the neglect of a son.

10

The military tradition of the Cummings stretched back to Dewey Cummings, son of a peasant farmer who, wrongly accused of murdering his father's landlord, the Baron of Bolton, escaped to Liverpool and then stowed away to Boston. The year was 1773 and Dewey Cummings was twenty. Two years later, when the American War of Independence broke, Dewey Cummings was among the first volunteers. He fought the British in Lexington at the start of the war and, having risen to Sergeant-Major by the end of the war, he had the pleasure of standing in the company of George Washington at Yorktown as George Washington accepted the British surrender.

William Cummings, grandson of Dewey Cummings and great-grandfather of Anthony Cummings, continued the military tradition when he joined the confederate army in the American Civil War. But he wasn't as fortunate as his grandfather. He was blown to pieces on the second day of the Battle of Gettysburg. He was only twenty-five. Nevertheless, fifty-five years later, the Cummings' military tradition became firmly established when Roberson Cummings, the father of Anthony Cummings, returned home from World War I a decorated Lieutenant-colonel, praised for his bravery and command in battle, including the heroism of his fighting battalion at Chateau-Tierry where they had helped the French slow down the German advance.

Besides the living presence of Anthony's father, the pictures of the uniformed soldiers lining the walls of the living room—the serene painting of his great-great-great-grandfather after he returned from freeing the nation from the evil of empire, the photograph of the youthful arrogance of his great-grandfather just before he left to do battle against the evil of human bondage, and the imposing, army-decorated photograph of his father upon his return from freeing the world from the evil of tyranny—would not allow Anthony to forget his family's military tradition. The pictures imposed their will not only on the living room but on his sense of duty. When Anthony was growing up, it seemed to him that these men had taken upon themselves the godlike task of ridding the world of injustice: they had been all that stood between light and darkness; they had been singly responsible for keeping evil at bay. The three pairs of unflinching eyes seemed to follow Anthony even when he left the living room, imploring him to always do the right thing, to stand-up against evil wherever it surfaced.

Growing up, Anthony couldn't think of any more glorious an occupation than that of a soldier; he couldn't think of any better arena in which to battle evil than the army. His family had helped to free the nation, free its citizens and free the world.

His opportunity for continuing the family's military tradition, for combating evil, the evil of genocide, Nazism and Fascism, came in 1941 with the Japanese attack on Pearl Harbor. Then, a second year engineering student at Washington University, Anthony gladly laid down his books and exchanged the university for the army. But with his consignment to the tiny Caribbean island of St. Lucia, where he was to help build and maintain an air force base, his enthusiasm and excitement quickly dissipated. Wasting away on a barren rock in the Caribbean Sea, far away from the action, from the seat of the evil he was supposed to be fighting, wasn't his idea of being a soldier. When he had first enlisted in the army, his dreams were of facing the enemy squarely (in Europe or Asia), of eradicating the evil from the face of the earth, as his ancestors had done in previous wars, and of returning home as heavily decorated as his father had returned from the previous world war.

In spite of Anthony's disappointment, his respect for the army was too deep to allow him to protest his assignment or to ask for a different one. The army commanded and he obeyed.

He arrived in St. Lucia on July 4, 1941, and became engulfed in the construction of an army-base and a lookout post in the southern fishing and agricultural village of Vieux Fort. He and his fellow American warriors transformed the canefields and pastures on the outskirts of the village into a patchwork of secondary runways, and, in building the main runway, they changed the course of the Vieux Fort River to flow in a more easterly direction. They further transformed the village's surroundings by punctuating the landscape with circular mounds of earth, the inside of which served as camouflaged hangars. They built a military hospital, where soldiers injured in Europe where treated enroute to America. They transformed Moule-A-Chique, a bold promontory jutting into the ocean and forming the southernmost part of the town, into a lighthouse and radar station, and on its western side they built a dock to accommodate war and cargo ships.

By the time these constructions were completed, Anthony had long set aside his dreams of glorying in battle and had fallen in love with the island: its many stone-strewn rivers in which barebreasted women did their laundry, the twin peaks the islanders called Gros and Petite Piton that stood like virgin breasts; the warm and boiling pools of slate-black sulphur-water at the base of these Pitons; the many verdant mountains that seemed to follow and engulf one everywhere one went; the people, their simplicity, the delight they took in living in spite of their poverty; the women, ebony-black Negro women, copper-brown Indian women, simple, unspoilt, refreshing as a drink of spring water on a hot tropical day.

So when the war in which he had fired not one shot ended, still enchanted by what he called a tropical paradise, the land of the gods, Anthony wasn't quite ready to return home. With the permission of the army, he had stayed on until 1949, the year the army deactivated the base. By then, though he knew he would greatly miss the island, Anthony was looking forward to returning home. Since the day of the city's death by fire, he had been feeling uneasy and listless. It was as if he had done something wrong and some kind of punishment lay in wait. He had interpreted this state of mind as time to go home.

Upon his return to St. Louis, his hometown, Anthony took advantage of the G.I. bill and returned to Washington University to complete his degree. There, he met, fell in love with and married Lynne Miller, the daughter and the youngest of three children of a well-to-do Boston family of Quaker roots.

While Anthony had grown up revering the past and his family tradition, Lynne Miller had taken delight in upsetting her parents' conservative sensibilities. She went out of her way to make black friends whom she brought home just to shock her parents. She made a point of listening to jazz, blues, rock and roll, the kinds of music her parents considered banal. She embarrassed her parents when they had guests by speaking in street vernacular. Unlike her brother and sister who had been happy to attend Harvard University and study Law and medicine, Lynne wanted to study music, something her father considered useless. But worse, she wanted to go to an out-of-state college. Her father had disagreed vehemently and threatened not to pay for her education. But, in her determination to be different, to be non-traditional, Lynne was as stubborn as her father. Eventually, they arrived at a compromise. She would attend St. Louis's Washington University but she would have to study something more useful than music. So Lynne decided on a double major—music and accounting.

To Mrs. Miller, her daughter's only redeeming quality was her passion for cooking. Lynne tried all kinds of recipes and created many of her own which her friends were only too happy to copy. Cooking was as much of a creative outlet for Lynne as was poetry to others. Cooking was the only thing traditional about her. When Anthony had first asked her out to dinner, she had proposed instead to cook for him. That night she had tried one of her new recipes. Anthony hadn't complained about her cooking then, and hasn't complained since.

Upon graduation Anthony got a job with the United States Corps of Engineers, while Lynne taught music at St. Louis's St. Mounts High School. In spite of Anthony and Lynne's best efforts, they were to remain childless, and, as if to fill the void of child-lessness, the couple threw themselves into one social cause after another. They made regular donations to charitable organizations like the United Way and the International Children Relief Fund. Lynne became a dedicated advocate of the feminist movement and joined a local feminist Chapter. Both Anthony and Lynne were vehemently opposed to segregation and racism. In 1960 they became paying members of the NAACP, and on May 12, 1964, they marched with Martin Luther King in Chicago.

When the Vietnam War began, Anthony broke away from two hundred years of family tradition, and passionately opposed the war. He pronounced the war an evil against humanity. And for the first time in his life he began to question the morality of war and American Imperialism.

With the Cummings holding such liberal views on so many issues, and with Lynne always welcoming opportunities to show-off her cuisine, their home, located in University City a couple of miles from Washington University, quickly became the place where feminists, black sympathizers, antiwar protesters, critics of U.S. imperialism, and high-minded blacks met to thrash-out the issues of the day, to masturbate their egos, and to enjoy Lynne's cuisine.

But as the sixties rolled to an end, leaving in its wake the assassination of Martin Luther King, Malcolm X and J.F. Kennedy, the Cummings became increasingly disillusioned and despondent with life in America. It was then that the pristine beauty and simple life of St. Lucia that Anthony had enjoyed so much during his army days began to beguile him. He suggested to his wife the idea of retiring early to St. Lucia.

Though Lynne had thoroughly enjoyed the island during their honeymoon, and with her inheritance and their pensions they had more than enough to live on, she was skeptical. She wasn't quite ready for a life of leisure. No matter how beautiful, it was one thing to spend a week or two on a two-hundred-thirty-eight-square-mile, one-hundred-thousand-people island with no museums, no theaters worth talking about, and cinemas that played mainly karate or antiquated movies, but another to spend the rest of your life there. So it was only when her husband said, "we could open a restaurant and bar," did Lynne show definite interest. She had always harbored the wish of owning a restaurant where she could offer to the world some of the dishes she had concocted over the years. She would have the best gourmet restaurant on the island, she thought. So in the middle of 1972, while the Watergate story brewed, the Cummings completed their plans for moving to their island paradise.

11

Past midnight, Robert and Trevor, now in their early twenties, unwillingly left the "pit" of Clarke Cinema, and were already missing the shouting, the swearing, the dirty jokes, and the calling across the darkness of the cinema of nicknames like *Fouk-Sal*, dirty crotch, *Lapo-Cal*, penis-skin, and *jock-fair*, masturbator. The dollar each of them had paid to sit in "pit" had been more than worth it. They couldn't think of any better way to spend a dollar. "Pit" was seven rows of benches without back support at the front section of the cinema immediately in front of the movie screen. For fifty cents more they could have sat behind "pit," in "balcony," on back supported benches, away from the sweat, congestion, and vulgarity of "pit". And if the benches of "balcony" were too hard for their buttocks, and too close to "pit" for comfort, they could have paid a dollar more and sat on cushioned seats in "box" at the back of "balcony." But to sit anywhere else but "pit" was to miss all the fun: to miss the shoving, the fighting, and the lewd jokes; to miss finding out who was fucking whom, who was cheating on whom, and whose mother was a *jamet*; to miss showing how, after the movie, one was going to fuck someone else sister or mother; to miss farting loudly and smelly and laughingly pass the blame onto one's neighbor; to miss the chance of parading and acting out one's favorite actors on the stage below the movie screen before the movie trailers came on. So besides an unwillingness to pay more for something they could get for less, they, Robert especially, would not have gone anywhere but "pit". The happenings in "pit" were part of the package, part of the night's entertainment. In "pit" Robert was in his element. He was the very embodiment of "pit."

Outside, the vendors who earlier crowded the front of the cinema, selling sweet drinks, malta, roasted peanuts, chewing gum, sweet biscuits, oranges, mangoes, apples, ripe bananas, turnovers, coconut jam, and much more, were gone. Still occupied with the sword fights, the hand-to-hand combat, and the blood-spills of the double-feature karate movies they had just seen, Robert and Trevor silently crossed Micoud Street, turned left on Bridge Street, and walked along side the large showcase windows parading the best of what J.Q. Charles had to offer the people of St. Lucia. That is, those willing and able to pay. It was a week night, a Thursday night, so save for the occasional loner and movie goers returning home, the streets of Castries were empty and quiet.

Midway across the show case windows, unable to contain any longer the excitement and tension of the karate movies, Robert suddenly screamed, "yaaaa," and using the showcase window as his movie screen he theatrically attacked Trevor with a deadly combination of sidekicks, karate chops, and punches.

After symbolically blocking the fury of Robert's attack, Trevor, imitating the Silver Fox character of the first movie of the night, fell gracefully into the crane stance. He balanced himself on his left foot, lifted his right leg with knee pointing out, spread his arms sideways like the wings of a crane, and cupped his hands inward to form a beak-like weapon. With front kicks and hands that had become beaks, he was ready to counter attack. Watching the bird poised to attack, Robert burst into laughter. Despite the bird's menacing stance, he reminded Robert of Christine, the woman he once wished was his mother, the woman with whom he was now secretly in love, the woman he adored. Acknowledging that his crane stance was funny, Trevor joined in the laughter. Still laughing, Robert patted his one and only friend on the back, and the two headed for the Conway, their common destination.

They turned right on Jeremie Street, then left on the John Compton Highway. To the right, under the shade of the market, several homeless men, oblivious of the pungent stench of the market and two nearby drains, were sound asleep on cardboard beds. Inside the market, outside of Robert and Trevor's sight, a stray cat was tracking a mouse who had been feeding on scraps of decaying pork intestines. The inseparable friends didn't witness the chase, neither did they hear the squealing pain of the mouse as the cat's paws landed on, and broke its back bone. To the left, Port Castries and the Caribbean Sea. Several cargo ships dwarfing the city lay at anchor. Guiding both ship and airplane, the light of the lighthouse at Vigie point glistened on the Caribbean Sea.

As they passed the market, they were distracted by a solitary figure stumbling across John Compton Highway. They knew her well. Rosa. She was drunk on all nights except the one night a week she joined the swarm of women that loaded bananas onto the banana boat like ants scurrying with food to their colony. And even then, she took two shots of white rum before braving the banana-loading toil. In light of all that white rum, Robert and Trevor often wondered where she got the strength to carry bananas. But they didn't concern themselves too much with that. What they needed her for required little strength. In fact, any absence of strength in her was to their advantage. They knew her route well. She would pass behind the market, pass the Marketing Board, cross Darling Road, pass through the Gardens, and cross over Chaussee Road to get to the one room shack she lived in, situated in the back yard of a friend who, for the sake of earlier and happier memories, took pity on her. But she only made that trip when she could. On some nights, too drunk to walk, she slept under the shade of the market, or made it as far as the gardens.

"Look who goes there." said Robert. "Dread, we're in luck tonight." And grinning like a kid about to receive candies or shirly biscuits, Robert warmly wrapped his arm around Trevor's shoulders, squeezing his friend's shoulder as one would squeeze the shoulder of a woman. But he wasn't about to receive any candy, he was about to take it.

Trevor forced a grin. His heart wasn't in the direction his friend was about to take him. But as countless times before and in various circumstances he reluctantly followed Robert's lead. He mutely followed. The past had taught him that it was futile trying to talk Robert out of whatever devilment he had set his mind to.

Robert knew that his friend was always reluctant to go along with his exploits. Some people always need a little coaxing, a little help, he reckoned. He knew what would help. He released Trevor's shoulders, took out a joint from a cigarette packet, fired it, inhaled long and deep, then passed it to his shadow. His shadow performed the same ritual and passed it back. This was their third joint for the evening, for they had smoked two joints before going to the cinema.

While smoking, they kept an eye on their quarry. To avoid alerting her suspicions, they allowed her to cross the street, and then followed some fifty yards behind. She wasn't hard to track. Drunk and stumbling, she moved at a funeral pace. Ever so often she stopped, swung her arms around as if warding off evil spirits and mumbled something akin to magic words not even she could understand.

Robert didn't mind the delay. The quest was just as thrilling as the conquest. He now had a one track mind. He was a cat tracking a mouse, a tiger stalking a deer. But his hunt was much easier than that of either the cat or the tiger. Civilization was asleep. This night belonged to him. Castries had turned jungle, a concrete jungle. He took another long pull on the joint and passed it to Trevor.

Trevor wanted the whole thing done with as soon as possible. In fact, he wished they had continued to the Conway which, when they first saw Rosa, was less than two hundred yards away. All the while they were tracking Rosa and smoking the joint, he was building his resolve. He was saying to himself, "not this time. No Dread. This time I mon going to say no. I eh going to take part in this abomination, this wickedness, anymore. Not this time. No sah. I don't care what he says, I eh going through with it."

He was even thinking of discontinuing the tracking, and heading back to the Conway. But like in the past, and in countless other situations, he was afraid of losing esteem in the eyes of his de facto father, of losing the friendship of the big brother he never had, of losing the attention and affection of the person who, since the age of five, had given his life form and direction. The attention and affection he once craved so much from his mother who was too beautiful to care and too busy to notice. Besides, Robert showed such a great need of him.

True, after the Christmas Eve theft of Colletta's money and the two nights in jail, he had avoided Robert for two months. But after two months, the same needs that had first drawn them together on that first day of school, eight years before, drew them together again. And then it was like there had never been a separation. Robert continuing his exploits (stealing fruits from fruit stalls at the market, shoplifting, stealing neighbors' hens and cats for beach cookouts, lifting batteries and other car parts for resale, and now he was pushing grass at soccer matches, at the cinema, at "blockos", at dances) and Trevor going along reluctantly.

Nothing will change tonight. Instead of parting company with his shadow, right then and there, Trevor pulled on the joint and told himself that he would accompany his shadow but he would not participate.

They stalked her. She entered the darkness of the Gardens, where the city lights did not penetrate, and they closed in on her, quietly. Robert pounced on her and grabbed her by the arm. In her drunken stupor she turned around as if wondering what evil had accosted her in spite of her magic words and the warding off of evil spirits with the swing of her arms.

"You are under arrest," said Robert, and he dragged her to the secrecy of a corner of the garden underneath a flowering flamboyant tree. The sweet scent of the flowers permeated the garden.

"What?" she mumbled.

"You are trespassing."

She vaguely remembered that it was only a few days ago that she was arrested, and the jail had smelled the same as today, like perfume and flowers. She had never imagined that jail would smell so sweet. And she wondered why the police were so strict, arresting her for passing through a garden. After all, she hadn't touched a thing: not a mango, orange, banana, grapefruit, or coconut. She wasn't partaking of any forbidden fruit. At least none that her alcoholic haze allowed her to remember.

He forced her down on top of the fallen flowers, on top of the leaves. She heard the crunch of the vegetation under her, felt the dampness, smelled perfume mixed with the musk of earth and decaying vegetation. Then a sharp pain between her legs made her forget all other sensations. He had entered her violently, as violently as he had entered all the women he had slept with. It didn't matter whether the fruit was offered to him or, as now, he had forcefully taken it. The pain cut through her white rum haze as the white rum had earlier cut her throat. She winced and wondered: what have I done that my punishment is so severe? I was just trespassing, I didn't take any fruit.

But it had nothing to do with her. Her only crime, if one could call it a crime, was intoxication and defencelessness. Rape or no rape, this was how he had entered all the women he had ever entered. This was why he had never had a relationship that lasted longer than a month, why he was now reduced to drunk, defenseless, white-rum-reeking Rosa.

The women who weren't drunks and defenseless talked

among themselves. So the word got around. At first, each woman he slept with thought that it was because he had been overly excited that he had entered them so quickly and had pumped away so rapidly and so violently. Entered before they were wet and ready, before any foreplay, before any sort of caress they could speak of. But they soon found out that there was nothing better to look forward to. No tenderness, no caring words, beyond what was necessary for their clothes to come off. The women might have been willing to forgo orgasms, if only there was a hint of caring and a few strokes of tenderness. But not much of that was forthcoming. They sensed that there was nothing loving about bedding him, nothing to differentiate between their love making and two strange dogs fucking; except one is done in secrecy and the other in the open. So after at most four weeks of awkward walking, of little better than rape, they left him and avoided him as they would a nest of wasps. Sometimes they quickly hooked up with another man just to make sure their message to him was as clear as was his brutality.

The women sensed right. There was nothing loving about his love making. When he fucked, he wasn't making love. He was using his weapon to hit back at the world, back at his mother whom he hated, back at society for looking down on him, for calling him wharf-rat, vagabond; back at his neighbors for condemning him to jail, to the gallows. His hatred, whose source he didn't understand nor cared to understand, was concentrated in his weapon, the weapon with which he waged war against women and therefore society.

The women sensed right. They got smart, and passed the word around and soon Conway women and beyond stayed clear of him. So Rosa, the woman he had used initially to rid himself of his virginity, had become one of the few remaining receptacles into which he could release his hatred.

He pumped so hard and so violently, that it only took a few minutes. He grunted, convulsed and released his venom into the world. He got up and pulled up his jeans. She, thinking her jail term was over, was trying to get up. He pushed her back to the ground and said, "stay down, *salòp*." Then he called Trevor, "hey Dread, she's all yours."

Before Robert's grunts had ended, Trevor had already gone through the same transformation that had allowed him to join Robert in raping Rosa for the first time five years ago, and since then had enabled him to bed other women. Before then, other than Christine, his own mother, he had no interest in women. Christine, in all her high-life and fast-life would have never imagined that her son's unmet childhood craving for motherly love and affection had turned into a more serious craving; the son she had always considered a burden, a hindrance to her enjoyment of life.

It was six years ago in May, the hottest month of the year, and at midday, the hottest hour of the day, that Trevor first experienced this transformation that made the raping of a deranged woman, reeking of white rum, palatable. That day he had just arrived home from school for his lunch when he heard grunts and moans coming from his mother's bedroom. When he peeped through a crack in the wooden partition separating his mother's bedroom from his, he saw the sweating, perfect body of his mother twisting and moaning under another body not so beautiful, but sweating more profusely. His anger and feeling of betrayal rose into a bulge in his pants, and the bulge grew painfully unbearable. So having recently learnt the secret of masturbation from Robert, he took out his bulge and proceeded in earnest, his stroke matching that of the stranger on top of the beautiful body. He stroked with such intensity, that although the stranger had a head start on him, they came at the same time, and, to Trevor, it was he and not the stranger who had come inside the beautiful body. Since that day, that hot day in May, all he had to do to masturbate, to bed another woman, or to rape the white-rum-reeking Rosa was to imagine that he was entering the beautiful, sweating, twisting, moaning body of the midday heat of May.

When Robert announced that he was done, Trevor was ready. The joint had helped, the darkness and the flowers also. They made it easier to conjure the perfect, perfumed body of Christine and not the alcohol-reeking, deranged woman who thought she had been arrested. He entered, not like his friend, but gently and slowly, like a groom his virgin bride. He came to her so lovingly and caressingly that in her drunken stupor the policeman on top of her had become her man, the one she once loved more than herself, the one who only had to say the word and she would die, kill for, the same one who ten years ago had abandoned her for another, after which she had tried twice to kill herself. The first time by slashing her wrist with a razor blade and the second time by drinking what she thought was gramazone. After two attempts at a quick, sudden death, she had resigned her self to a slower, but surer method, a method that guaranteed success. The only thing she had not bargained for was this constant police harassment.

The policeman was so gentle, that she fell asleep on the damp bed of sweet-smelling flowers and decaying leaves. The gentle, love-making policeman became her lover, and the garden her bedroom. The policeman who had turned gentle, and the garden-jail that had turned into a flower-smelling bedroom.

"Dread, what's taking you so long?" Robert wanted to know. But his question fell on deaf ears.

Several minutes after Robert's inquiry, Trevor responded. He cried, "Mama, Mama," and he released into his sleeping mother all the love that he craved from her which he never received. But as always she paid him no mind. She was deaf to his desperate spasms of love. He got up, zipped his jeans, brushed the dead leaves off his clothes, and then the remorse began, the same shame and remorse that overwhelmed him after each time he had allowed Robert to talk him into one mischief after another. Like in the past, as he walked alongside Robert to their common destination, he vowed never to do a thing like that again, not only that thing,

144

but some of the other crooked dealings that Robert was getting him into.

Robert was cheerful and relaxed. He had just released his venom. His tension was gone. He said, "did you see how she moved under me? That *jamet* was just begging for my dick. What took you so long, Dread? Did I hear you cry Mama? It was that good-ah?"

"Mon, we have to stop that crap. We go end up in jail one of these days, or worse the gallows. See what happened to us when you went and steal that old woman's money. Lucky for us we were under age, but next time go be a different story. We should begin by getting jobs and stop that "pushing" business." replied Trevor.

"Dread, you are starting to sound just like my mother and that crazy woman, Coletta. Don't dig nothing, Dread, we safe. No Bylon worrying about a *woumier*, drunkard."

Hunched like a sentry over the city, Morne Fortune, the sight of many battles between the French and the English in their lust for the land of the gods, looked down in silence upon the sleeping woman, ravished with white rum, venom, and love misplaced. Morne Fortune, like the sleeping city, had answered the woman's cry of pain with silence. Untrue to its name, Morne Fortune had brought the woman no fortune.

While the woman slept her drunken sleep, the friends continued to the Conway, their common destination, in silence. It was past one. Except for stray dogs, nothing stirred. The night was dead.

145

12

At nights, especially, the Piton, situated on Morne Fortune and overlooking the Cul-de-Sac Valley to the south, the Caribbean Sea to the west and the red-roofed city of Castries to the north, seemed well suited for romance. Hanging glasses and lined bottles of Cockspur, Mount Gay, Vodka, Hennesey, and more, add color to the soft dim lighting. It was one-thirty on a Saturday night. Soft reggae music filled the empty spaces of bar and mind. Outside, most of the city was asleep. But for the occasional interruptions of fireflies, the Cul-de-Sac valley lay in total darkness. The lighthouse at Vigie illuminated the calmness of the Caribbean Sea.

Christine was seated at the bar. She was wearing a tight, red, leather miniskirt, a yellow bodice not quite reaching her skirt, and showing off her upper chest. Her hair was brushed back, but was loose and flowing. Her lips had been touched with pink lipstick; this was all the makeup she was wearing, but that was all that was needed. Not a blemish could be found on her copper-brown skin.

She was not alone. Seated besides her was her escort, Keith Polius, owner of a chain of hardware stores and a member of the Chamber of Commerce. Two seats away was Rasak Habib, a Syrian by birth and owner of several clothes stores. Next to Rasak was Vernon Myers, a criminal lawyer and a member of the opposition Labor Party. At the opposite end of the bar from Christine was Mitchell Pierre, a math and economics teacher at the A-level college. Behind the bar, keeping their customers' glasses filled, were the owners, Anthony and Lynne Cummings.

Except for Christine and the Cummings, it wasn't a quiet gathering. On the contrary, tempers were rising, an argument to remedy the problems of the island was heating up. Christine was smiling through it all. A raised eyebrow to express doubt or lack of understanding, parted lips and enlarged eyes to register shock, a soft chuckle to say this was funny, a nod and quiet eyes to say I understand, were the extent of her participation. Yet somehow she was the center, the focus of the rising tempers. Unaware to the men, the island's problems were just pretexts for each of them to say to her: "I am smart; in the days when we roamed the plains of Africa, I would have been head hunter; I am the only man here worthy of your attention."

Oblivious to the ambience of the Piton, but emboldened by the warmth of Christine, Keith was the loudest and the most passionate. Vernon had just stated his main thesis for the night, that the UWP party was a party of and for the rich. Nothing angered Keith more. Especially after what happened last week when two youths entered his store on the Boulevard, acting like they came to buy something. Then as the cashier opened the cash register to give a customer change, the youths, one looking like a *douglah* and the other as black as Keith, thrust their hands in the cash register and ran away with handfuls of cash. Keith gave chase, but he was no match for the youths and the streets were crowded. They got away. But what burned Keith even more than the money was that, instead of people grabbing the youths, they were calling: "run boy, run." It was as if he were the enemy, the criminal.

Keith went on the attack. "Vernon, don't give me that rasta crap about the UWP is a government of the rich. The problem with St. Lucia is pure and simple: the people are too damn lazy."

"I won't go as far as to say that people are poor because they are lazy," interrupted Rasak. "But as my father always use to say, he has never seen hard work kill anybody. Look at me. I came to this island with only a suitcase to my name. Day in and day out, I went from door to door, selling merchandise. I was the object of much ridicule. Some people never paid for the clothes they took on credit. Yet today I cannot say that I have done badly."

Keith hardly listened to Rasak's support. Since the robbery his anger had been building up. St. Lucians and their laziness had occupied his mind. How they thought that it was the duty of the government to put food on their tables. How they sat on their backsides all day long, watching the streets, watching other people's business. Some calling themselves rastas, but this was yet another excuse to smoke dope, rob people's gardens, loiter on the beach and street corners and hassle tourists and passersby. How Lucians had no discipline, no work ethic. The few that worked for him acted as if they were doing him a favor. It was as if they were on a go slow. Attending to customers came second or third to chitchat, or to doing their nails. How they didn't seem to think that their livelihoods depended on the success of the business. It was as if someone was forcing them to come to work; as if he, Keith, was the slave driver and they the slaves, so it was their duty to sabotage his business.

But before Keith could further vent his anger, Christine said, "how old were you when you first arrived here, Rasak?"

Rasak was taken aback by the unexpected question. They were discussing politics, not his personal life. The soft voice, the smile that always seemed to be saying more than it was saying, jolted his memory to another girl back in his hometown in Syria, the one all the neighborhood boys, himself included, were after; the one he had never touched, but who still penetrated his dreams. She was the most beautiful girl in the village, yet she was nothing compared to the woman of the soft voice and the smile that seemed to be saying more than it was actually saying.

"I was twenty-five. No, make that twenty-six. Yes, I was twenty-six years when I got here."

Christine wanted to ask, why had he left Syria in the first place to come to little backward St. Lucia? But Keith would wait no longer.

"People look at people like myself that have worked hard and sacrificed so much for the little we have and they call us exploiters, bourgeois, Babylon. Yet, it is people like me, people like Rasak, here, that are building this country, that are holding this country together. Without people like us this country would fall flat on its ass. So, tell me, how can we go forward with that kind of attitude, that kind of mentality. Laziness, not the government, is the cause of this country's poverty."

Keith's eyes spread open with fire, staring at each man seated at the bar, daring them to challenge his position. Keith then lowered his gaze to his scotch-on-the-rocks, swirled his glass, and cooled his throat in preparation to attack the rebuttal he knew was coming.

Christine looked up to him, smiled a smile that seemed to say "how manly you are," and tenderly squeezed his arm. But she was thinking: men and their loud talk, the beating of their chest, their big ideas that almost always amount to nought, that never change anything. And all the while what they are really looking for is someone to quiet their boyish fears, their fear that in the passion of the night their members would go limp. No matter how many times they fuck, how many women they fuck, there is always the fear that the next time, the next woman, they will not be able to perform. So they keep on chasing women, and their fear of going limp keeps chasing them like their fear of death. Instead of beating their chest and fighting over big ideas that change nothing, why don't they focus on the practical things, the things that make life more comfortable, more enjoyable; things like eating on time, getting a full night's rest, dressing good, making sure clothes match, maintaining friendships, the little things that add up to a life.

Keith's talk of laziness annoyed Vernon to the extreme. It took him back to England when he was there studying for his law degree. On a warm summer afternoon, he was taking a stroll in his neighborhood when he came across an elderly, white couple working on their lawn. He greeted them and they engaged him in conversation, asking him where he was from and then about life in St. Lucia. They offered him beer and he sat on the porch with them, talking and drinking. At some point in the conversation, when they were discussing the economy of St. Lucia, the woman said with serious conviction that the islands were poor because the people were lazy. Now, he could have told her about how the British have ravished and exploited the people and the resources of these poor islands, but he didn't. He was in a compromising situation. After all, he was in the people's country, sitting on their porch, drinking their beer. Instead, he told them that he has never seen anyone work harder than a St. Lucian banana farmer. No one can accuse them of laziness. He described to them the rivers, the mountains, and the valleys banana farmers had to cross to keep her grocery stores stocked with bananas.

Yet here was Keith, his own countryman, repeating the same nonsense that the white woman had said to him twelve years before. Back in London he had been in a compromising situation, but now he was in his own country, a first class citizen, buying his own drink.

So before Keith could bring his glass to his lips, there was loud clapping and all eyes switched to Vernon, and soon Vernon's claps gave way to a hoarse voice.

"Keith, I have never heard so much bull-shit in my life. Because you have acquired a few stores and you have a few people under you, don't sit here and tell me we are poor because we are lazy. Go to the docks on banana day and see how the women, like ants, load the banana boat. Go to the country with a farmer, watch him carry hundred pounds of fertilizer; see how many banana trips he makes over hills so steep and slippery that you, without any load, would find impossible to climb. Go to sea with one of those fishermen, and when you return, if you return, tell me if it is a lazy occupation."

"So what you think? I acquired my stores by sitting on my backside?"

"That's not what I'm saying."

"So what are you saying?"

"I'm saying that this UWP complaint about the people are lazy is just an excuse for them to continue to ignore the needs of the masses, while bit by bit they give the island away to foreigners. Like giving Geest the people's bananas for next to nothing; giving foreigners tax exemptions to build hotels; guaranteeing loans for foreign businesses, some of whom run away with the money, while there are locals dying for loans to start businesses."

Anthony had heard the same arguments by the same people many times before. Soon after he and his wife had opened the Piton Restaurant & Bar in May1973, the Piton had become a place of rendezvous for Peace Corps and other white foreigners seeking comfort in numbers, for expatriates with lingering memories of the big countries, and for local politicians, businessmen, lawyers, doctors and government bureaucrats seeking to promote and solidify their status. In the five months the Piton had been opened, he had acquired more knowledge of the politics and economics of the island than had many St. Lucians in a lifetime. The ongoing debate was a recycle, but he couldn't say the same of Christine, the woman of the magnetic beauty, the woman accompanying the man speaking the loudest. No matter how many times he looked at Christine, it was as if he were seeing her for the first time. So instead of listening to the men inflate their egos, he was enjoying Christine as he had done from the first time Keith had proudly brought her to the Piton. She reminded him of his military days at the Vieux Fort Airforce Base. She rekindled a yearning in him for the Indian and black girls he used to fuck. Christine made him miss the full round buttocks of the black girls and the coyness and hairiness of the Indian girls. In Christine was the best of both races. Since the Saturday night when he first saw Christine, more and more, when he was fucking his wife, he would imagine that it was Christine he was fucking.

Christine, who knew men better than men knew themselves, who knew immediately when a man lacked self-confidence, who could smell a man's sweat before he perspired, had not failed to notice Anthony's lustful eyes and sly smiles. She was amused and slightly intrigued. She was yet to fuck a white man and she wondered what it would be like. She considered Anthony old, but he was in good shape. He took a four-mile run on the beach every morning. Each time she caught him looking in her direction, she narrowed her eyes slightly and gave him half of that smile that said more than it was saying.

Christine swayed gently to Bob Marley's: *I don't want to wait in vain for your love.* Vernon ordered another rum and coke. Lynne replenished his glass. He took a sip of his drink, and before he could take a second sip Keith took the floor.

"Yeah, yeah, blame people's backwardness on the government. Where would this country be without the UWP, without Compton? Before the UWP took over, this country was literally in darkness. Running water and electricity could be found only in the coastal villages, kerosine lamps and flambeaus were the norm. Outside of the main towns and villages, health centers were non-existent, malaria, T-B, and bilharzia were rampant. Secondary education was for the fortunate few. This country has a lot for which to thank the UWP."

No matter how many times Lynne had listened to these political discussions, she always paid rapt attention. Saturday night, after the restaurant closed and the crowd at the bar thinned out and the conversation changed from friendly banter to heavy social, political, and economic discourse, was the high point of her week. Lynne was thinking that no matter how much things changed, some things never changed. Her home in St. Louis had been a focal point where like-minded people met to thrash out the vexing issues of the day. Now, though several thousand miles away, the Piton was serving exactly the same purpose. As Keith ended his defense against Vernon's rebuttal, Lynne's attention shifted momentarily to Christine. She watched Christine swaying in a dreamlike state to the music. Unlike her husband and the men at the bar, she wasn't impressed with the child of the gods. She dismissed her as vain, superficial, and lacking any substance. The woman was only concerned with how she looked and how to get men to spend money on her. Lynne wondered why a man like Keith, a prominent member of the community, could leave his wife and children at home and carry that slut all over the place. Lynne would have been shocked if she were to uncover the thoughts her husband was harboring for Christine. She would have been even more shocked if she had known that the woman she labeled "slut" was the child of the gods.

"Tell me," replied Vernon, "if the government has done such a great job, why are our people suffering from malnutrition, living on a diet of bread and butter and green figs. Why are so many of our youth roaming the streets, sitting around street corners, unable to find jobs? Why do our secondary schools turn away hundreds of students each year, reducing them to a life of menial labor? Prices are skyrocketing and merchants like you and Rasak keep getting richer at the people's expense. You say the youths are loitering, stealing, hassling tourists. Tell me, what are they to do without jobs, without schooling? This government better watch out. I tell you. It is these type of conditions that give rise to coupe d'etat, to communist takeovers."

Christine glanced at Mitchell. Something about him bothered her. Not once since the three months she had known him had he shown an interest in sleeping with her. She couldn't say the same of the rest of the men gathered around the bar, or for that matter, of most men she had come across.

Mitchell wasn't untouched by the glitter in Christine's eyes and the smile that had every man at the bar thinking that the spark in her eyes was just for him and that, even though she was with Keith, if he were to play his cards right, he might be the lucky one, the one who would share her bed tonight. All except Mitchell. He wasn't lusting. Christine wasn't his type. He liked his women black, blacker than black; those who were so black that their skin shone like the eyes of Christine. He was living with just such a woman. He wasn't lusting. Sex wasn't his main preoccupation. He liked to have a steady woman so when he felt the need he didn't have to go hunting. His woman at home was more than enough for him. Teaching, instilling black and national pride in his students, gathering around a bar, as tonight, and discussing politics, economics and culture were his passions. He considered himself an intellectual, a philosopher. But for his radical views and his tendency to criticize the government and the business class, he would have long been the headmaster of the A-Level College.

Mitchell had developed the habit of painting light skin women black and then seeing whether they were still beautiful. This was to make sure that he didn't pronounce a woman beautiful just because she had straight hair and light skin. He didn't want to get trapped into that slave mentality, that slave legacy. Many such women people considered beautiful had failed his beauty test. Sipping his fifth Guinness for the night, he applied the test to Christine, as he had done each time he had found himself in her company, and, as before, she passed without question. Yet he wasn't lusting. He wasn't tempted. He was admiring her beauty as an art lover admired a masterpiece that cost way above his means.

The same could not be said of Vernon. Like Keith, Rasak, and Anthony he was married. Nevertheless his desire for Christine was untamed. Tonight as he looked at Christine's pink lips he could almost feel them encircling his penis. He asked himself for the hundredth time: "what will I have to do to get this woman?" Three weeks ago he had tried to get her to spend a weekend with him in Barbados. Her response was that smile of hers that drives a man wild, and: "What would your friend Keith say? I'm not sure he would like that."

Keith, as if aware of his friend's designs on his mistress, went on the war path again.

"You have finally shown your true colors. So that is what you are trying to get at all the time. Get rid of democracy. Take people's hard earned property and give it to bums who have never done an honest day's work. Nationalize everything. Well, brotherman, let me know when you are planning to take over, so I can get the hell out of this country."

Mitchell swallowed the rest of his Guinness and ordered another. Foam spilled over as Lynne opened the bottle and slid it over to him. He allowed the Guinness and his thoughts to settle. He thought that none of them has touched on what was one of the biggest ills of the country—the shopkeeping disease. The first thing people think of when they were contemplating opening a business was buying and selling. From the poor old women sitting at stalls to the J.Q's and M&C's, everybody was buying and selling. Those who were actually producing something, manufacturing something, could be counted on his fingers. And if he happened to pass by any manufacturing concern, he could rest assured that it was largely foreign owned—the banks, Winera, Heineken Brewery, all the major hotels, Cable & wireless, on and on. With all the money those large retailers had been piling up over the years, why were they not investing some of it in hotels, food processing plants, clothes factories, etc? He knew that the Agriculture Ministry's food processing laboratory at Union had developed a number of processed foods. All that was needed was for businesses to set up processing plants. Yet as far as he knew no one had come forward.

Mitchell took a swallow, and allowed his thoughts to spill over. "One of the biggest problems we face in this country is that we are a nation of shopkeepers. Rasak, instead of importing all the clothes you sell, why don't you buy some machines, get some tailors together, and open a clothes factory? Keith, you sell furniture, so why don't you buy the necessary equipment, hire some joiners and open a furniture factory?"

"Listen to the professor. Listen to the professor," said Keith, laughingly.

"This is no joke," responded Mitchell. "Take tourism, for example. Do you know, since most of the hotels are foreign owned, without high taxes on the hotels and on the goods and services that the tourist use most, it is unclear that tourism produces a net benefit to this country?"

"Teach, teach," said Vernon. "Tell them about the huge tax breaks these foreign-owned hotels are getting, and tell them about all the profits they send back to their home country."

"That may be so, replied Rasak, but the hotels create plenty of employment."

"True, tourism creates employment, but, with all the major hotels owned by foreigners, and with inadequate taxes on the hotels and other tourist facilities, tourism may still be producing a net loss. Besides, if the objective is to increase employment, there may be better ways to do so than tourism. But this is not my main point. My point is, if instead of just buying and selling, some of our people invest their money in hotels, tourism would be of much greater benefit to this country."

"What is wrong with stores, what do you have against stores?" asked Rasak? "After all, the objective is to make money, so making it buying and selling seems as good as any other. Money is money."

"In one sense you are right, but in another sense you are wrong," replied Mitchell. "Let me tell you where you are wrong."

"Tell him professor," interrupted Vernon.

"There are two main problems with buying and selling as opposed to manufacturing. Buying and selling involves very little value added, therefore it doesn't add much wealth to the economy. Instead, there is mainly a transfer of wealth from the masses to the merchants and to the foreign suppliers. Second, shopkeeping involves very little training, so it doesn't add much to the nation's stock of skills and thus contributes little to the country's long-run productivity growth and hence to wage improvements."

Bob Marley was stilling grooving away, but Christine had stopped swaying. For the first time tonight she was paying rapt attention to the ongoing discussion. But she wasn't evaluating or deciphering the logic of Mitchell's arguments. She was captivated by the tone of confidence in his voice, the calmness of his demeanor, the eyes that suggested that the spoken words were just a glimpse of the depth of knowledge and understanding that lodged in the larger than normal head.

"You are right in that as a businessman your objective is to make money," explained Mitchell. "Money made from buying and selling, from the hotel business, from manufacturing, is all the same money. So I'm not blaming you businessmen for focusing on shopkeeping. After all, if conditions in the economy are such that shopkeeping is the enterprise that produces the most profits for the least risk, businesses would be stupid not to focus their efforts on buying and selling."

"It sounds like you are biting your tongue, professor," said Keith. "A while ago I thought you were going to get rid of us merchants, now a sudden change of heart?"

"No. The blame lies with the government, not the merchants," continued Mitchell."

"The government, the government," replied Keith. "It always comes down to the government. Why don't you all Laborites, and you all communists give Compton and his boys a break?"

"Listen, listen," said Mitchell. "It is the high custom duties that the Government has in place that has turned us into a nation of shopkeepers."

"Take him to school, professor. Take him to school." said Vernon.

"These custom duties, which sometimes amount to twice the purchase price, take away the only alternative consumers have to the exorbitantly priced goods of retailers. The end result: the large retailers earn large, secure profits, making alternative sources of investments unattractive. If the government were to drastically cut down on custom duties, you would soon see our large retailers investing in hotels, food processing plants, and garment and other factories, creating better quality jobs and greater wealth."

"This is exactly what I have been saying all night," said Vernon. "The UWP is a party for the rich. They squeeze the little man, so that the rich can get richer. The merchants, the chamber of commerce, are making a killing from skyrocketing prices. Teach them professor, teach."

"How about you lawyers? I have heard no one say that you all work for peanuts. On the contrary, I have heard plenty of stories of how lawyers like you swindle people out of their land," replied Rasak.

Christine caught Anthony looking at her again. As she returned his look, he quickly diverted his eyes. Christine smiled. The smile made Anthony wonder if she would accept an invitation to come to his house when his wife was away. Sometime soon his wife was planning to spend a weekend in the Mabouya Valley with a graduate student from the University of Florida who was conducting research on the role of women in St. Lucian agriculture. That weekend would be perfect for inviting Christine over. He glanced at her again, and he realized that she had been expecting him to look again, because she was waiting with that smile of hers. Is she teasing me, or what, he wondered?

"So professor, is that what your party, what's its name? Yes, The Progressive Forum, that disguises itself as a discussion group, intends to preach when it finally comes out from undercover and declare itself a political party—get rid of the businessmen, close down the hotels, nationalize everything, turn the country into a communist state?"

"I'm suggesting no such thing," said Mitchell.

"This is exactly what you saying," said Keith. "But you forgetting one thing, professor, this is a small country, getting enough business to stay afloat is a precarious affair at best. And don't forget the custom duties are one of the few sure ways government has of raising revenues to pay people like you. So when you get rid of custom duties, how are stores supposed to stay in business? Where will the government get money? How is the government supposed to meet its financial obligations, especially since you all guys are forever holding the government hostage over pay raises?"

"Where will the government get money? Let me tell you where." said Vernon. "They will get plenty of money when they stop filling their pockets and when they stop exploiting the poor for the benefit of the rich."

"Vernon I'm not talking to you anymore. I'm talking to the professor here. Every time I turn my head the professor and his teacher's union are on strike, and the government is giving them a back pay. The same government that already has problems coming up with enough money to pay civil servants. I tell you, if the government were to follow his advice, stores would go out of business "black-is-white." There would be widespread unemployment and shortages of every kind. This is the problem with you college boys. You all are out of touch with reality. The government wastes its precious few dollars sending you all to university, and when you all come back, what do you all do? You all want to revolutionize the system, change the government, turn the place to communism. The very same government that is paying you all fat salaries just to sit on you all backsides all day philosophizing."

"Pay him no mind, professor," said Vernon, "he is just jealous of your education. This just goes to show you that no matter how rich a businessman gets, he always feels a bit regretful and insecure about not having gone far in school."

"Give me the money, any day, any time, and keep your education", replied Keith. "After all, it was to make money, to get a good job, that you all went to university. Most of you all can't survive one day without the government. Take the professor here for example. He has a degree in economics, business, and whatever else, so why doesn't he put all that economics to good use, start a business, create his own employment, and in the process create jobs for other people? But no. This isn't radical enough for him. Instead, he goes up the Morne and fills the heads of the people's kids with radical nonsense. I keep on saying, but you all don't listen, without us storekeepers this country would fall flat on its ass."

"Pure nonsense," said Mitchell. "If you all close shop there will always be people waiting in the wings to take over. Because, even if the government reduces custom duties, there will still be plenty of profit to be made. But what will happen is that, since profits in retailing would no more be so much out of keeping with what other enterprises are earning, people would start taking a more serious look at other forms of businesses."

"Well professor, tell me when you and that "Forum" of yours are going to turn this country into a communist state so I can get the hell out." said Keith. "In the meantime, brothermen, the man have some other business to take care of, and the lady here is beginning to yawn. Goodnight."

"Goodnight everyone," said Christine in a voice as soft as the lighting inside the Piton.

Keith and Christine walked out into the night, and the bar fell into an audible silence. Soon everyone was leaving. The prize was gone. There was no more reason to lengthen the evening.

While they went to their sanctuaries, the gods of the land marveled at the naivete of humans. They said to each other, "humans are so vain, they think that they are in control of their fate, their destiny. They keep talking about free will, but they are puppets on a string. Their folly time immemorial. If we were to tell these fools that were seated here tonight that the poverty they have been discussing is a direct result of the curse we have cast on the land, they would laugh us to scorn. So let them wallow in their own delusions, inflate their egos, and suffer the consequences."

13

"So you were in St. Lucia during the war?" asked Christine.

"Yes," said Anthony, "I was stationed in Vieux Fort. I helped build the base and some of the other military installations."

"Were you gone by the time of the fire?"

"No, I was still around. In fact, I helped put out the fire."

"I remember that fire. It's a pity you Americans didn't come sooner. This was the worst experience of my life. We lost everything."

"Yeah, that fire was something. Then Castries looked like Hiroshima."

"When did you return to the States?"

"I went back not long after the fire. I might have stayed longer, but since the fire, something kept bothering me. I don't know for sure what it was. But I had this strange feeling of having done something wrong and some kind of punishment was in store for me. That feeling stayed with me weeks after the fire. Worse, on some nights I dreamed that my quarters was on fire and I couldn't escape, I couldn't move. Finally, I decided it was time to go home."

"Someone must have placed obeah on you. Maybe the father

162

of one of the girls you soldiers used to fool around with," said Christine with a giggle.

"It surely felt like obeah."

"Talking about girls, there is another thing. That afternoon, after we put out the fire, there was a girl no older than sixteen standing in the crowd. Her hair was in disarray and mingled with ashes, coal marks were all over her clothes, and she looked like she had been working all day in a coal mine. Of all the people in the crowd, she looked the most wretched. But strangely, her miserable condition seemed to accentuate her beauty. She was just as beautiful as you. I have forgotten her face, but the look that was in her eyes, I can never forget. Every time I see you this girl of the fire comes to mind."

"Maybe it was me, and fate has brought us together. Do you believe in fate?"

"No, I don't. I think each person decides his own fate. In life one makes hundreds of decisions, large and small, but each decision pushes one further down a path. It is the choices we make that decide our fate."

"Why did you come back to poor St. Lucia? Oh, I know. All the time you were away you've been dreaming of all those Indian and black girls you left behind. Come to think of it, you probably left plenty children behind."

"No, No," laughed Anthony. "I am in love with this island: the people, the beaches, the mountains, the small streams, and yes, the women, especially *douglah* women. Did I say it right, *douglah*?"

Christine laughed with abundance. The laugh and her eyes were saying "I am almost ready."

"Pretty soon," she said, "you will be speaking better patois than me."

"This calls for another drink," said Anthony. And he left for the kitchen to get more ice to mix their fourth round of drinks for the afternoon.

Lynne was away visiting her American student friend in the Mabouya valley for the weekend. Thursday, at lunchtime, Anthony had waited for Christine outside the law office where she worked. She had been surprised to find him there waiting for her. But her smile suggested that the surprise was pleasant.

"Mr. Cummings what you doing here, do you need a lawyer?" she had asked.

"No," he answered, "I came to see you."

"Moi?" she teased, her head cocked sideways, her eyebrows raised high, her pretty mouth opened wide.

"What are you doing Sunday?" he asked, brushing his hand across his forehead as if wiping off perspiration.

"Nothing in particular, but Sunday is a long way off."

"Why don't you come over Sunday afternoon at around two for a few drinks?"

As if staring into a bright light, Christine looked at him with squinted eyes. "Why, you having a party?"

With her eyes narrowed and focused on him, Anthony felt like she was seeing right through him. He shifted his weight from one foot to the other, and apparently not knowing what to do with his arms, he alternated between folding them, brushing one over the other and fiddling with keys in his pocket. "No, not exactly. Just a few people."

He is acting just like a boy, thought Christine."Will your wife be there?"

"Yes, of course."

"Should I tell Keith, he may want to come?"

"No, you know him. He always gets into a heated political debate. I want it to be a quiet, relaxing afternoon."

"O.K. I'll be there."

"Good," said Anthony, brushing his hand across his forehead, "let me get back to the Piton."

That was Thursday. But right now, feeling nice and pleasant, Christine smiled as she thought of how this old white man had lured her into his house. The house was just five houses away from the Piton and its balcony faced the Caribbean Sea. The shade of two mango trees and a gentle sea-breeze shielded the balcony from the brunt of the afternoon heat. Leaning comfortably on the balcony, Christine looked down toward the sea over homes with yards interplanted with bananas, flower plants, mango, breadfruit, and plum trees that thrived on Castries's hot and humid climate.

Upon arrival two hours ago, Christine hadn't been amused when she found out that Lynne wasn't home and there was no sign of anyone other than Anthony. Her first impulse had been to walk out. But Anthony had been so apologetic and looked so harmless that she hesitated. And then her curiosity about this old, white man took over, and as the afternoon deepened and the rum and coke started its magic she was thankful that Lynne wasn't home. A while back she had noticed that Lynne didn't care much for her. That hadn't surprised her, though. She had come to expect women, especially married ones, to treat her coldly. With Lynne out of the way, she loosened up and became herself, the self that the most religious of men would find irresistible.

Anthony returned with the drinks. Christine asked, for the third time, "what did you do with your wife?" But this time there was no sting in her voice. No more sting than the gentle breeze blowing across the balcony.

"What can I say to make you believe that my wife had to go to the Mabouya Valley on short notice?"

"You crafty old man!"

Grinning, Anthony handed Christine her drink. She held the glass with unsteady hands. Some of her drink spilled on to the floor. He gently kissed his glass against hers and said, "let us drink to friendship."

"I drink to crafty old men," she said with a lingering laugh.

"Tell me about your people," said Anthony.

"Well, where should I start?"

"Start with your grandparents."

"My grandmother was from India. Her mother-in-law tricked her into coming here as an indentured servant. As soon as my grandmother set foot on land, they sent her to work on the Forestierè Estate. There she met and married my grandfather. At sixteen my mother got pregnant for a black man, my father. So six months pregnant, my grandfather kicked my mother out of the house, and a year after I was born my parents moved to Castries, and I became a city girl."

"Your turn, crafty old man."

"I am from a military family. My great-great-great-grandfather stowed away to America from England."

"How many greats was that?" teased Christine.

Chuckling, Anthony told her about his family's military tradition, his own military days, how he had fallen in love with St. Lucia, and what had made him decide to come back.

"But you haven't told me anything about your wife," said Christine. "How did you meet her?"

"I met her in college, after I returned from St. Lucia. On our first date she cooked dinner and after that I was all hers."

"So the saying is true, the way to a man's heart is through his stomach?" said Christine.

Anthony smiled in response, locking eyes with the child of the gods. Under the influence of the rum and coke, the child of the gods glowed with an unsurpassed sensuousness. Anthony felt clothed in an ocean of sensations. The child of the gods smiled, all knowing, intensifying Anthony's desire to unbearable heights. They stood close, unaware of time. His hand traveled up her arm to her shoulders. He rested his glass on the balcony, and began to massage her neck and shoulder muscles. He felt her delicate bone structure and watched tension leave her shoulders. She moved her neck to the rhythm of his fingers. No one had ever massaged her so sensuously. He felt her leaning more and more of her weight onto his chest. He took her glass from her and rested it on the balcony next to his. She felt his hardness throbbing against her buttocks. She moaned softly as he continued to massage her back and shoulders. He turned her around and kissed her, her lips melting into his, their tongues playing a tango. As darkness began to circle the Morne, and a quietness settled on the city, he led her into the house, into his bedroom. He undressed her unhurriedly, then he undressed himself while she waited on the bed with her eyes closed. She opened her eyes to the sight of the body of a thirty-five-year old, instead of the sixty-five-year old body she was expecting. His throbbing member was big for a white man, she thought. He kissed her, and she closed her eyes again as he played music on her body, in the fading afternoon light.

He took his time, savoring the moment. Even when he knew she was ready to receive him, he did not enter her immediately. First, he rubbed his penis against her wetness. She writhed and twitched with pleasure. She wanted, no, needed him inside her. She held him at the waist and pulled him to her. He knew he shouldn't wait any longer. He parted her with his thumb and index finger, and entered her, inch by inch. Once fully inside he increased the tempo. That was exactly what she wanted, needed, because she had been more than ready. Soon every muscle of his thirty-five-year-old looking body contracted to propel every bit of his essence into her. She took it all in and mixed his with some of hers. At the height of her release, she held him so tight that his last thought before falling into a deep sleep was how could such a delicate body hold so much strength.

Half an hour into their sleep, they were awakened by the banging of doors and windows. They saw lightning and they heard rain, wind and thunder. It seemed to them that all the elements of the heavens had combined forces with the intention of destroying the house, destroying them. Despite the warmth of their passion, the lovers shivered. Anthony got up quickly to close the doors and windows. He returned and under the cover of the bed sheet he snuggled up to Christine, but the moment was gone; the storm had destroyed the magic. Suddenly, both he and Christine wished they were as far away from each other as possible.

They, Keith, Rasak, Mitchell, Venon Myers, and the Cummings, the group which the Saturday night crowd at the Piton invariably dwindled to as the night lingered, hugged the bar, nursing their drinks. Tonight Christine's absence was as palpable as the darkness outside, and as heavy as the Bob Marley tune, "No Woman No Cry," now pervading the bar. Unlike previous Saturday nights, tonight no voices rose with passion, the country's problems were suspended. Keith, the one who used to fuel most of the debates and whose voice used to grow the loudest was tonight the most somber. His face was grim and harried, his hair which was usually meticulously combed was ruffled, his eyes were bloodshot. For most of the night he stared into his glass which, no matter how quickly Lynne refilled, seemed always empty.

"I told her, I told her not to go to this party in Soufrière with those guys. They drink too much and drive too recklessly. But you know what she said?" Keith, looked up from his empty glass at his comrades, as if he were seriously expecting an answer. "I'll tell you, I'll tell you. She laughed. Serious. She laughed and she said: 'Don't tell me you jealous. You jealous.' And she laughed that laugh of hers. So I said no more."

"It is a shame,"said Rasak. "a real shame, that one so beautiful, so full of life, should die so young. Such a shame."

"Yeah, it's a real pity," said Mitchell. "One minute one is here, and the next, one is gone. Life is a real trip."

"If she had only listen," murmured Keith. "If she had only listen."

"This Soufrière-Castries road is a death trap," said Vernon. "It's high time the government do something. It seems like every year somebody loses his life on these precipices."

"You know," murmured Keith, "I would have done anything, anything, for that woman. I know you all will not believe me when I say I loved this woman more than I loved my wife. But it is true, it is true."

"Brother, I understand completely,"said Vernon. "This was a special woman. There was none like her. A special woman, that's what she was."

The bar fell silent again. A silence interrupted by the swirling of drinks. A silence as palpable and as heavy as the absence of Christine.

"It isn't just a problem of bad roads," said Anthony, breaking the silence. "People drive much too fast and reckless. The police need to enforce traffic laws more diligently. They should do like in the States: impose stiff fines, take away drivers' licences, and let some people spend a few days in jail."

Anthony spoke the words, but to him they sounded dull, hollow and hypocritical. For in his heart he knew that it was his infidelity, his lust, that was the culprit. Since the afternoon of passion, the Sunday afternoon, two weeks ago, when he was brought back to his days at the Vieux Fort military base in such a rupturing fashion, the feeling that he had done something terrible and was about to pay for it was many times stronger than at the time of a city's death by fire. Since the afternoon of passion, his dreams had become a confusion of fire, smoke, and suffocation.

Lynne didn't share the remorse of the men sitting at the bar; she was a bit sorry that the girl had met such a fate, but she couldn't conclude that the girl didn't deserve it. Frankly, she wasn't surprised. The girl wasn't much more than a high-priced prostitute. Fast lives end sadly. Now married women can sleep more soundly. The wife and children of that Keith can now see more of him.

"I went down to Soufrière at the site of the accident," said Keith, almost to himself. "I have never seen a car wrecked so badly. The car left the road and rolled all the way down the precipice to the sea. The bodies. The bodies were smashed, smashed I say, smashed beyond recognition. If she had only listened."

The other men at the bar couldn't conceive of a Christine smashed beyond recognition. They couldn't envision the flawless, copper-brown skin bruised and crushed. They couldn't picture a Christine without the smile that always made one feel that one stood a chance and that any day now one would be the lucky one. They couldn't imagine that the eyes that always seemed to say more than they were saying were now saying nothing. The men could accept, though barely, the abstract notion of Christine being dead, but not being crushed beyond recognition. They heard Keith's rumble, but it didn't penetrate their alcohol haze. Each time Keith spoke and the men looked toward him they half expected to see Christine beside him, smiling that smile of hers. Not even Mitchell, the only man in the room that hadn't lusted after Christine, was immune to this unwillingness to see Christine as anything but the beautiful woman that used to sit across the bar from them. Several times tonight, in the silence of his Guinness, Mitchell had applied his beauty test, and, besides himself, had come to the conclusion that there was none more beautiful than this *douglah* woman, and there probably would never be.

"When is the funeral?" Asked Rasak?

"The funeral, what funeral? Yes, the funeral, the funeral. This afternoon I went up Forestierè to inform her family of her death. The grandmother, grey, wrinkled, and bent double, insisted on keeping the funeral up at Forestierè. 'If it is the last thing I do, I will bury my own.' This was what she said. The funeral is Monday."

This was the second time that Valda, the woman sold into servitude by her husband and mother-in-law, eighty-one years ago, had insisted that her Castries offsprings be buried close to home, be buried at Forestierè.

The first time was 1958, the year that Julita, Valda's daughter, the daughter who Valda's family and village had abandoned, had banished, died of a death that had lasted four years. A death that began on a Monday morning in September when Leonce,

Julita's husband and Christine's father, a farmer turned fisherman, went to sea. That day the farmer turned fisherman and his crew didn't return in the afternoon as was customary. The people were alarmed. After all, this was the hurricane season. None of the other fishermen who had been to sea that day had seen the crew. Leonce and his fishing crew were lost at sea. Three days passed, no sign of Leonce, nor the two other crew members, nor the fishing canoe. The people were sure. The fishermen had received a death by water. This wasn't the first time that fishermen had gone to sea and never returned, and the people reckoned this would not be the last. Yet Julita, the woman who had already been promised, but whose love for Leonce had cost her her world, remained hopeful. She remained hopeful for six months, because it was also true that sometimes the fishing canoes washed up on some neighboring island, St. Vincent, Martinique, for example, or got picked up by an ocean going vessel. Like the fishing crew from Vieux Fort who had been lost at sea and ran out of fuel. Six weeks after they left the shores of Vieux Fort, a Venezuelan vessel had picked them up at the mouth of the Amazon River. By that time there was very little flesh left on their bones, their skin were blistered beyond recognition, and their hair scorched to a fiery red. Coconuts and other edibles floating down the Amazon was what enabled them to stay alive. But all the while they were at the mouth of the river they thought they were still in open ocean. It was only when the Venezuelans informed them otherwise that they were able to explain the floating coconuts. So the woman who had exchanged her world for the love of the farmer turned fisherman, now lost at sea, remained hopeful. But after six months her hopefulness ran out. She had given up her world for love, but now the love was gone. There was nothing left. The zeal of the young woman who had braved the wrath of her family, her village, her world, and joined her spirit, the spirit of India, with the spirit of Africa, had dried up. There was nothing left. So Julita turned to a slow death, a death by the bottle.

She lost interest in baths, in clothes, in her hair. For a while she continued to make bakes, dalpouri, turnovers, and fish cakes to sell at the wharf and at bazaars. But what people a short time ago couldn't get enough of had become just about inedible. It appeared that even if she were to pay people to eat her food, they would not have touched it. In fact, her body odor and her rum-reeking breath were more than enough to keep people away from whatever she was selling. Soon Julita stopped cooking altogether, neither to sell, neither for herself. Rum, white rum, seemed the only thing in which she was interested. Christine, her daughter, begged her to move in with her. But the woman who was left with nothing, didn't budge. For four years she lived off of white rum, the occasional meal Christine brought her, and scraps from her neighbors' kitchens.

So when Christine found her mother dead on a Tuesday evening, with an empty bottle of rum lying next to her, she wasn't surprised. Her scream which caused the neighbors to interrupt their dinner and come running, wasn't out of surprise or shock. Her scream was from the despair that came with the thought that now she was all alone in the world.

Before Christine had reached her fourth birthday, she had already lost her father's parents and his brothers and sisters to a death by precipice. On the way to the Sulphur Springs for an all day outing, the bus carrying her father's family and some other people from Babonneau plunged over a precipice just before entering Soufrière, when it tried to avoid a speeding car. In one day, one hour, one minute, one second, her father's family was wiped out. Wiped out before she was even of an age to know them. And just four years ago she had lost her father to a death by water. So now her father's side of the family was non-existent, was wiped out as clean as a blank page. And then, she had just lost her mother, lost her mother to a death by the bottle, a death by design. Her remaining family, the only ones she had left, her family on her mother's side, had abandoned, discarded, disowned, banned her even before she was born. And as far as she was concerned they couldn't care less whether she was dead or alive. So when Christine found her mother, for all practical purposes, her only remaining kin, her only remaining link with the past, lying still beside an empty bottle of white rum, she let out a scream, a scream announcing to the world that she was now all alone.

The coroner who came to check the cause of death wrote, "death by intoxication," but Christine and the neighbors knew that alcohol had nothing to do with Julita's death. Julita had given up her world for love. The love was gone, so she was left with nothing, and nothing from nothing left death.

On the night of the death of her only daughter, Valda had slept miserably. An inexplicable cold seemed to have entered the very core of her seventy-eight year old bones. No matter how many blankets she pulled over herself, the cold remained. By five-thirty she had had enough of fighting the cold, of trying to sleep, so she got up, opened her door, watched the slow defeat of night, and listened to her rosters announce the break of day. Sitting in her doorway, welcoming the dawn, she was much warmer than she had been all night under her layers of blankets.

At six o'clock she turned on the radio, and returned to her seat at the door. And then it happened—the early morning news. A woman answering to the name of her daughter and of the same age had died last night of alcoholic intoxication. Valda grew weak, and the cold that had destroyed her sleep returned. Trembling, she pulled herself off her chair to wake up her husband who had been oblivious to her predicament during the night. "Wake up." she said. "Our daughter is dead, she is dead, I said, dead." Then she sent word to her sons who had seen their sister many times by the wharf, but had never once said hello.

"We have to get her up here. We have to bury her here," Valda told her husband.

"Woman, she has been dead a long time ago. She killed herself when she turned herself into a whore, sleeping around with that *neg*. Let them bury her," replied the husband.

"She is alone. The *neg* you talking about drowned several years ago. Don't you remember four, five years ago, three fishermen got lost at sea and never returned?"

"Woman, let me be. Let them bury her."

Suddenly, Valda's frail body heaved with anger. "You denied me my daughter when she was alive, you are not going to deny me her now she is dead."

"Do whatever you please, woman. What does it matter, anyway? It is not like I remain much time in this life. Let me be."

Four hours after Valda heard the news, she, accompanied grudgingly by two of her sons, left the heights of Forestierè and descended to Castries to claim the daughter she had denounced while alive.

When she arrived at her daughter's house, Christine and the neighbors had already begun preparing the dead for burial.

"This is my daughter," shouted Valda, as soon as she entered the house.

Voices stifled in mid-sentences, and all heads turned around to find out who owned the voice that had suddenly proclaimed possession of the dead, as if someone had contested such ownership. Christine and the other women in the house saw a frail woman, well on her way to being bent double, grey hair, grey eyebrows, skin of unfinished leather, and sharp, piercing eyes emitting a passion more apt for the living than for the dead.

"I gave birth to her, and I am the one who is going to bury her," proclaimed Valda.

"Grandma," called Christine, tentatively. She was seeing her grandmother for the first time. "Grandma."

A tear rolled down the parched face of Valda. Christine went to her grandmother and kissed her on the cheek. She was not alone, after all.

Later that day, after Julita had been placed in a coffin, and Christine and Trevor, and Valda and her two sons had accompanied the coffin to Forestierè, one neighbor speaking over her fence to another neighbor recounted the meeting with the grandmother.

"I tell you, the old woman just about accused us of taking her daughter away from her. And her two sons stood there on alert as if ready to fight for their dead sister—a *woumier* no one would give a farthing for even when she was alive."

"Isn't it they themselves that kicked her out of the house, out of Forestierè, just because she got pregnant for a black man? And now she is dead, they acting as if she is made out of gold."

"Yeah, these Indians think they are too good for us. But during the past four years, after the death of her husband, not even dogs would come close to her."

"Maybe the father was saving her for himself, or maybe to offer her to the devil, but since she lost her virginity, to a black man especially, she wasn't of any use to either the father or the devil."

"You really think they offer their children to the devil?"

"Since when you became stupid? How you think the Indians of Vieux Fort and L'Abbaye got their wealth."

On Monday afternoon Julita was buried. During the all night wake that followed, in which the people drank coffee and rum, retold folk tales, and danced to the sound of drums and quadrille, mothers told their daughters, "take this as a warning. See what happens when you forsake your own and instead join the disgusting negs." The message would leave an indelible mark on the memories of their daughters.

This second time, upon the death of her granddaughter, Valda, now ninety-four, was too old to make the trip to Castries. She couldn't walk unaided, and even then she had to stop and rest every few steps. Her eye sight and hearing were only a third of what they used to be. Her voice was now reduced to a whisper. She was living with one of her sons. Her husband had passed away ten years ago. But Valda's physical impediments hadn't diminished her desire to have her own buried close to home. Her sons who themselves had already entered old age raised walls.

"For Christ sake, Mama, you don't even know her. Since that first time when she came up for her mother's funeral, she has only been back once to visit you. Why go to all that trouble and expense for someone who was little more than a stranger?"

If Valda heard the objections of her sons, she didn't show it. When Keith arrived at her son's home in his almost new volkswagon and informed them of the death of the child of the gods, for once in a long time Valda's voice rose above a whisper, "Young man, we will bury her. We always bury our own." And then her voice returned to a whisper, "if this be the last thing I do, I will bury her."

So, in spite of her sons' objections, sixteen years after Valda went down to Castries and reclaimed her daughter, her youngest son (accompanied by his son and daughter) descended into Castries and brought back the broken body of her granddaughter. The granddaughter would be buried next to the grandfather who had banished his daughter six months pregnant with the granddaughter.

It was a windy Monday afternoon. It was a windy funeral. The wind, having no respect for the dead, seemed set on separating the mourners from their somber clothing. And it was as if it didn't want the mourners to hear the words of the priest, because it carried the words of the priest away from the mourners to the blackbirds, flocking the surrounding trees. To be heard the priest had to speak louder than he did at Sunday Mass.

Among the mourners were the inner circle of the Piton Restaurant & Bar—Anthony, Lynne, Rasak, Vernon, Mitchell, and Keith. Unlike the wind they paid their respects: dark clothing, flowers on the grave, condolences. But except for Lynne, they were hypocrites. They still couldn't accept that the dead was truly dead, that the one who had been the focus of their many nights at the Piton, the one whose presence had justified their late night sessions, and had provided the attraction that glued them into an impromptu social club, was no more, was smashed beyond recognition. The wind unclothed their hypocrisy: they paid their respects, but they were yet to believe that the dead was truly dead.

The two inseparable friends were there too. The eyes of Robert, the one who once wished Christine was his mother and later his lover and had befriended her son as a substitute for her, were as red as the eyes of one who had been swimming all day in the ocean, but it was hard to decipher whether the eyes were red out of anger, rage, sorrow, or weeping. But there was no denying that the eyes of Trevor, eyes that were now rivers of tears, were the eyes of one in deep sorrow, a sorrow for love denied, love that never was, love unrequited. Love for a mother who had paid him little more attention when she was alive than as she lay dead in her coffin. After the priest had uttered his final prayer for the dead, and the first shovel of dirt splattered on the coffin, Trevor suddenly attempted to leap into the grave. Luckily his shadow was right next to him. Robert grabbed him just in time, and wrestled him to the ground.

The grave covered, Valda, supported by two of her grandchildren laid flowers on the grave of the granddaughter whom she had seen only twice in her lifetime. Returning home, the wind threatening to disloge her black hat, Valda suddenly felt very tired. She couldn't remember when last she had felt so tired. Her vision receded, her knees buckled, and she slumped forward. Her grandson carried her home to her bed. There she remained for two days and on the third day she was dead.

14

On July 4, 1974, Castries was a breezeless furnace. The sun blinded the eye and scorched the skin. Asphalt on road surfaces melted and bubbled. Even with shoes on, walking the streets was like walking barefoot on coals. Water from the few standpipes that had not dried up was scalding hot. Many sought the cool comfort of the beach, but on this day the beach was anything but cool. The ever present sea breeze had for once vanished. The sand on the beaches burnt the feet like fire. The sea was almost as hot as water from the standpipes.

The two inseparable friends were among those who sought relief at the beach. Like night prowlers, all afternoon they smoked grass, listened to reggae, teased each other and slept intermittently under the shade of sea-grape and sea-almond trees.

Now the inseparable friends were seeing even more of each other. Shortly after Christine's death, Robert had moved in with Trevor. Christine's death made the move possible, but it was Felina who hastened the move. Late one afternoon, Felina came home to the overpowering smell of ganja. The smell set her blood on fire.

Twice before, she had warned Robert never to smoke ganja in her house. In fact, for this and other reasons she had kicked him out six times over the past two years, but each time she would take him back

Middle aged, Felina had become a bit more forgiving, she was now more willing to let the past remain in the past. Especially since Ralph, her other son, her real son, had done good by her, had made her proud. He had graduated from the St. Mary's College with eight GCE passes, all A's, and right now he was in Barbados, at the University of the West Indies, studying economics on Government scholarship. So she could afford to be a bit forgiving. She had something other than hatred to live for, and to give her life meaning. God had finally given her something for which to be thankful. She still didn't pray or go to church, and she never would, but occasionally she was willing to look up to the sky and admit that the sun was shining. Yet, if truth be told, it was to Robert and not to the sky that Felina should have directed her thanks. For it was the sight of policemen hauling Robert to jail, when he had stolen Colletta's money, that led Ralph to the resolution that from then on he would stick to the straight and narrow path, and he would make it a point to be the complete opposite of his brother.

So, as if sensing Robert's role in her younger son's success, in her greying years Felina could sometimes look at Robert without thinking of the betrayal, of the love that never was. Therefore, each time she put out Robert and he returned after a few days, adopting his best behavior, she would say nothing and let matters rest. Nevertheless, Robert would soon revert to his old habits and the situation would deteriorate, and before long mother and son would be cursing and insulting each other. So while Felina may have been willing to let the past lie low, Robert appeared to be doing everything in his power to revive it. Each time Robert came back, the confrontation got nastier. Cleaning the city's streets five days a week, loading the banana boat all night one night a week, and aging, were robbing Felina of her strength. Robert was beginning to walk over her. She had to put an end to it while she still could. She had softened in her mature age, but not that much.

This last time, her blood on fire, Felina opened the bedroom door to find Robert lying on the bed under a cloud of ganja smoke. She rushed toward him, screaming, and lashing out at him like an injured tigress. Still lying on the bed, Robert blocked her swinging arms, planted his feet just below her breast and pushed. Felina slammed into the bedroom wall.

"Watch who you hitting, bitch," said Robert, and he got up and went to the kitchen for a glass of water. Stunned, Felina stayed against the wall for a full three minutes. Then she got up and headed for the kitchen. She was sure about what needed to be done, what she should have done years ago, even before this curse, this animal, this *bouwo* was ever born. She passed by Robert who was seated at the kitchen table drinking water as if nothing had happened. She opened a kitchen drawer and grabbed a butcher knife, and without a word came at her son. Robert got up from his chair. His eyes moved from the knife to his mother's eyes. And an involuntary smile moved to his lips when he saw that the shine on the knife matched the shine in his mother's eyes. He looked at the knife again, then with the smile still on his face—the smile that seemed to be daring his mother to complete the act she had embarked on even before he was born, the act she attempted to enact each time she whipped him when he was a child—he held his mother's stare.

Her eyes shining with intent, burning with hatred; his eyes red, sleepish, smiling. As Felina came at him, for a brief second she saw darkness, tomblike darkness, and she couldn't breathe. Smoke was filling the darkness, and then suddenly there was a burst of red, of fire, and the fire turned into the pool of blood her mother had died in the night of the barking dogs. Then her mother's blood became her son's blood, the blood of the son she had hated even before he was born. Only this time it wasn't a landslide or coal-dust or one-hundred weight baskets of coal that had spilt the blood of her kin. It was her hand, the knife in her hand. Suddenly she again focused her eyes and saw her son standing one foot in front of her, transfixed, a stupid smile on his face, waiting with expectancy, willing her to complete the act she had embarked on. She stepped back from him as if he had some contagious disease, as if he were the one that wielded the knife. She placed the knife down on the kitchen counter. Her eyes lost their shine.

"No, I'm not the one that will spill your blood. Too late for that now. I should have done that when you were not yet. I will leave that for others. For the gallows. Get out of my house, and if you value your life, never set foot here again."

Robert continued smiling. He had won the war. He had finally defeated his nemesis. Besides, he was already planning to move in with Trevor. High as the gods of the land, he packed his things and sought the company of his shadow.

Now, on this unbearably hot July day, Robert once more sought the help of his friend. Throughout the afternoon he had been searching for the words that would convince his friend to join his plans for the night. He had to be careful. Since Christine's death, besides Trevor's familiar reluctance to join his escapades, Trevor had become religious, he had turned rasta.

It wasn't until four-thirty, when the sun was well on its way down, that Robert started on his well-used path of persuading his friend to join him in the night's adventure.

"Dread, you know those honkies, those Americans who own the Piton?"

"You know well I know them."

"Dread, from what I hear, those Bourgeois making a killing. Dem leave their big, rich country, and what do they do? They come to this poor country and exploit the masses, and siphon every little penny from the country. Dem are capitalist pigs. Is time that shit stop. They think they could fool us with their plastic smile: the grimaces dem pass as smiles. But in their own country they still subject the black man to slavery. I bet is the black power chase them out of America. When black man rise, nothing can stop black man. Dread, tonight we go show them, we go show them who this country belongs to. Today is Sunday, right. Guess what? All the money they made Friday and Saturday is in their house waiting to be placed in the bank Monday. Well, Dread, if we play our cards right, that money will never see inside a bank. Tonight the natives go take back what's theirs. Tonight is our perfect chance. They eh there tonight. This morning they went down to Soufrière where they spending the night. It's going to be a piece of cake."

"Dread, how many times I-mon have to tell you I done with stealing. I done with raping drunk, stinking, defenseless women. Why you think I went and get a job? No tanks, sah. It's here I-and-I part company with you. I-mon is a rasta now, none of that iniquity for I."

"Dread, give me a break. You call working for ADIS, going around spraying ditches, killing flies and mosquitoes a job? That eh no job for rasta. Dread, you dealing with poisonous chemicals. I thought rasta don't deal with chemicals. What kind of rasta you is? What I make in a few hours selling grass on the block is more than you make in a whole week."

"Maybe so, maybe so. But at night I can sleep easy. I-mon is at peace with myself. I can meditate with a clear conscious. It's time you give up your evil ways and step on the path of right-eousness."

"Rasta, you think those honkies righteous. They preach to us love thy neighbors as thyself, and next thing they enslave us, rape us, rob us blind. So don't give me that righteous crap. You know what I heard?"

"What?"

"I heard the old, stinking honkie used to fuck your mother."

"You fucking lying," said Trevor, and he suddenly jumped on top of Robert and they started to wrestle. "Take that back," he said. "Take that back."

Robert was pinned to the ground. Gasping for air, he said,

"ok, ok rasta, you win. I take it back. I was just telling you what I heard. I just the messenger."

"Who told you that?"

"Is Irvine, the guy from Lancers that works for the honkies. Dread, what has gotten into you? Let me go. Let me go before one of us get hurt."

Trevor released him.

"Dread, what I trying to tell you is let's make the honkies pay. Pay for everything. For four hundred years of slavery, rape, and exploitation that have continued to this day. Besides, them honkies full of money. Taking a few dollars from them is like taking a handful of sand from the beach."

"You sure they away?"

"Yeah, they away for the night."

"How do you know?"

"Dread, you not only turn religious, you turn lawyer too. Is Irvine told me. Ok? You satisfied?"

Midnight. Under the cover of darkness, two inseparable shadows crept up the Morne. The night provided no respite from the suffocating heat of the day. Castries slept restlessly. As the shadows approached the Cummings' residence, a dog barked. The shadows froze momentarily until they realized that their presence wasn't the cause of the bark. The dog was barking from a distance. The two shadows were sweating profusely. In contrast to Castries, the Morne was shrouded in darkness. A car was parked in the car porch.

"What is their car doing there, I thought you said they away?" whispered Trevor.

"Maybe they went with some other people. Who knows about those honkies? Just to take no chances we must be very quiet."

Casting furtive glances, Robert tried the front door. It was locked. He turned left and tried the door leading to the car porch. To his surprise the door creaked open. He switched on his flashlight, keeping the light pointed to the floor, and entered the house. Trevor followed closely behind. They passed soundlessly through the kitchen, through the sitting room, and entered a corridor. Then Robert stopped. There was a door on the right. Being so close behind and not anticipating the stop, Trevor stumbled into his friend. Robert swung his arm back and held Trevor to make sure his friend didn't fall and raise a racket. Settled, Robert slowly and quietly turned the door knob and gently opened the door just wide enough to peep in. It was the bathroom, they moved on. The second door on the right opened into an empty bedroom. The third door was half open. Moonlight shining through opened glass louvers revealed two bodies, stark naked and sound asleep. Their snores were barely audible over the noise of a fan whose breeze was turning the white, flowery window curtains into what, in the dim room, seemed like a dancing witch.

When Trevor saw the couple, despite the heat a chill ran though his body. He turned and started to walk out, out of the house, out of the night, out of this evil they were about to commit.

As for Robert, things couldn't have turned out more perfectly. Ever since Irvine had told him that Anthony, the old honkie, had been fucking Christine, he had been planning punishment. He knew very well that the Cummings would be home. Things couldn't be more perfect. Robert sensed the shift in Trevor's countenance. Even before Trevor started to turn around, he knew Trevor would change his mind. Just as Trevor shifted his feet to turn, Robert grabbed his arm and pulled him into the bedroom. The sleeping couple was oblivious to the scuffle.

Robert moved to the bed, he picked up a large ash tray sitting on the bedside table and smashed it with full force onto the right temple of Anthony. Upon impact the ash tray shattered, knocking Anthony unconscious. A trickle of blood rolled off his forehead onto his pillow.

The noise startled Lynne. Her head jerked up, but before she could make out the vague shape standing beside her bed, Robert was upon her. He sat on her back and pressed her head onto the pillow. While Lynne struggled, he turned his head sideways to see what his friend was doing. Trevor was standing there as if in a trance.

"Dread, what you doing standing there. This eh no movie. Take the flashlight, and get me some clothes to tie them up."

Trevor brought some pants and shirts. Lynne was still struggling. Robert grabbed and yanked her hair, and he slapped her viciously. "Quiet, *salòp*," he snapped.

"Dread, hurry up before the other *salòp* wake up. Hold her for me to tie her up." Trevor held Lynne down. Robert bound her feet and hands and then he gagged her. Next he similarly bound the husband. Lynne momentarily stopped her struggling to make sense of what was happening. She could make them out now. There were two of them. "What did they want? What were they after? My God, please don't let them kill us."

On top of the dresser was Lynne's jewelry box. Robert emptied its contents into his pocket. Then he and Trevor started searching for the money. They ransacked the bedroom, but found nothing. They exited the bedroom and entered the next room down the corridor. It was a bedroom converted into a study. Robert flashed the torchlight across the room. The back wall of the room was lined with bookshelves. Sitting on a desk was the inside tray of a cash register. Piles of money surrounded the tray as if someone had been interrupted in the act of counting the money. On the wall, above the desk, was a young portrait of Anthony and Lynne, a photo of Anthony in army uniform, and a photo of Anthony and Lynne in the Chicago Martin Luther King march.

"Dread, they knew we were coming so they left all this for us. Wait, I will be right back," said Robert.

Robert went to the kitchen and returned with a large paper bag into which he stuffed the money. They returned to the bedroom. Anthony had regained consciousness and was struggling to free himself. Robert punched him several times in the stomach. Anthony moaned in pain.

"Take all the money, take the jewelry, but leave us alone. Don't kill us," said Anthony.

Lynne was still struggling.

"*Jamet*, is hot you hot, is black dick you want. Well tonight is your lucky night." Robert pushed Anthony off the bed, untied the legs of Lynne and proceeded to ravish her.

While his wife was being violated, Anthony fell in and out of consciousness. Yet, through it all he had the vague sense that he was responsible. Because the feeling of having done something wrong and some kind of punishment was coming his way that had come over him soon after his night of passion with Christine had intensified with her gruesome death. So intense had been the feeling that Anthony couldn't make love to his wife. Each time he approached her he saw not his wife but the smiling face of Christine, teasing him, ridiculing him, ridding him of his manhood. At first Lynne had thought that her husband was cheating on her, but after keeping a close watch on him for a month, she had discarded that theory in favor of the alternate theory: her husband had suddenly gone impotent. All that running he does you would think he would last longer, she had thought.

As his shadow ravaged the woman, Trevor stood there transfixed. The blood he had seen trickle down Anthony's forehead had disturbed him more than even the anguished pleas of the violated woman. The trickled blood started his retreat. What the hell was he doing there, in the house of those white people? For one thing, he didn't need their money. Most fortnights his pocket change from the previous fortnight carried over to the next fortnight. So much so that often-times knowing he was going to get paid the following day, he gave his remaining pocket change to the guys at Clarke and Gaity who were always there fleecing. If he didn't need the people's money, what was he doing there? So what if the honkie used to fuck his mother, was that cause enough to enter his house in the middle of his sleep, rob him and rape his wife? His mother whom he never knew to be bashful about fucking. These honkies weren't the rum-reeking Rosa to whom he had lost his virginity. No, this wasn't Rosa who had nothing, no family that cared to claim her as family. These honkies were educated, rich, they rubbed elbows with all the bourgeoisie on the island. Not the kind of people you could rob and rape and get away with it. So then what was he doing there, in the people's house, when he should be in his own bed, or sleeping with his woman. He knew exactly what he was doing there. Robert had done it to him again. No. It wasn't Robert, at all. It was he. He had allowed Robert to talk him into this craziness. So when was he going to stop? When was he going to take back his life from the control of Robert? He who was approaching twenty-five, had no mother, and no kin he cared to claim or who cared to claim him.

Trevor heard the struggles of the woman, still pleading, though the damage had already been done, though she was no longer feeling the pain from the brutality of her invader. Trevor broke into a cold sweat, perspiration pouring all over his body. For suddenly he had a premonition, a vision, rather. A vision intensified by the window curtain turned dancing witch. He was lost forever. This act was going to be his last act. This was the crime, the abomination, that would make him pay for all of the other acts that he had allowed Robert to talk him into. This was the act that would end all acts. He saw himself hanging on the gallows besides his shadow, and there was a smile on his shadow's face.

Panic struck Trevor. But it was the contented, no, happy smile on his shadow's face and not the hanging that brought on the panic. Trevor's heart felt like a ton of iron was pressing down upon it, crushing it, and it started racing. He tasted bile. He was in a state of fright. The dancing witch had become a hangman.

The convulsive tremor of his shadow, and his shadow's grunts and moans as he released every drop of his final rage into the woman, propelled Trevor's feet to follow the speed of his heart.

So as if chased by the curtain turned dancing witch, turned hangman, he took flight. He ran out of the house, down the darkness of the Morne, then down the lamp post lit streets of Castries, down Bridge Street, past the police station, M&C, J.Q, the post office, right on Jeremie Street, past customs, port police and the fire station, left on The John Compton Highway, along the water front, past the stench of the market, the decaying Conway, the harbor, up to Vigie, and then right along the sleepy Vigie Airport, as if heading for Rodney Bay.

He ran not fully aware of where he was going. In fact, taking flight had not been a conscious decision at all. It was a reflex action, an instinctive action no different from that of a rabbit being chased by a dog. He didn't quite know where he was headed, but his subconscious mind was guiding him, much like an unconscious rider leaving it to his horse to get him safely home. His subconscious knew the setting, the place in the past from which he drew the most comfort, the most security. So with his heart pounding, his lungs bursting, he found himself on the beach at Choc. Once there, grabbing hold of his leg he bent down and vomited violently until it seems he would get rid of not just the contents of his stomach but his stomach itself. Then he cleansed his mouth with sea water, and lay flat out on the beach some distance away from his vomit. The cool, salt-laden breeze of the Caribbean soon stopped his perspiration and quieted his breathing. He lay there all night.

Back at the house, just as Robert had risen off from the ravaged woman and turned around to say, "your turn, Dread," he heard the door bang. "Dread, where you going?" He shouted. He rushed to the door, and risking discovery, yelled again, "Dread, where you going?" But for once his shadow didn't turn back, for once his shadow wasn't listening. "These Rasta's are all the same," he mumbled. "They full of talk, but no action. I tired of begging him. Let him go. I don't have any friends. I have never had a friend. I have never needed him. Now all the loot will be mine."

He returned to the house. They have seen my face, he reasoned. Yeah, they have seen my face. "Leave no trace," his mind directed. "Leave no trace." He tied up Lynne who was just about getting up, kicked Anthony some more, and went to the garage in search of fuel. There was a fuel shortage on the island so of necessity Anthony kept on hand a five-gallon can of gas. When Robert found the fuel, he mumbled, "see what I was telling the Dread? There is a gas shortage and here is this honkie, this exploiter, gobbling up the gas, depriving us of transportation."

With the gas and matches from the kitchen he re-entered the bedroom. He sprinkled gas first on Lynne then on Anthony, and then all over the bedroom.

"Stop. Stop," cried Anthony. "Kill me but don't kill my wife."

"Shut up, you honkie," shouted Robert. "No more exploitation, no more raping our people. Today is the day of judgement. Jah-Jah has spoken."

He moved to the door, lit a match, threw it into the bedroom and slammed the door close. Then with the paper bag of money in his hands and Lynne's jewelry in his pockets he left the house, quickly.

The burst of flames revived Lynne. Then she heard the laugh. The same laugh she had heard last Sunday at the foot of the Pitons. She and Anthony had spent the day in Soufrière. After they had soaked in the Sulphur Springs, the sore of the gods, Anthony got adventurous, and decided they should climb Gros Piton. Less than a hundred yards up, a stone dislodged under Lynne's foot, and she fell and strained her right ankle. In a few minutes her ankle had swollen to the size of a cricket ball. As Anthony lifted Lynne to carry her back to the car, she heard a laugh.

"Did you laugh just now," she asked?

"No," said Anthony.

"Did you hear a laugh at all?"

"No, maybe it was a bird you heard."

"Maybe." But Lynne had remained unconvinced. The laugh had lingered in her consciousness all week. Since then she had made sure her husband locked all the doors before they retired for the night. But tonight Anthony had overlooked the car porch door. Lynne heard the laugh, and she understood. She was right after all. She had heard a laugh last Sunday at the foot of the Pitons. As the fire raced toward her, the laugh grew louder, filling her being, and she saw a light shining between the Pitons, as in a tunnel, and she gave her self to the light, to the Pitons, to the gods of the land.

The fire reminded Anthony of another fire. The fire of a city's death. And then he saw the girl. The girl of a city's death by fire who looked like she had just come from a coal mine. He could see her eyes, the eyes he could never forget, the eyes that had driven him out of the island. And suddenly the wretched, coal-dust-covered girl was transformed into the most beautiful woman he had ever laid eyes on. When he looked closer, he saw that the woman was no other than Christine, and right in front of his eyes, in the midst of the fire, Christine undressed and was smiling, teasing, laughing at him, and a glow brighter than the flames surrounded her, and her breast grew larger and larger, until they became the Pitons. Then he knew. The girl of a city's death by fire was none other than Christine. She was right, after all, thought Anthony. There is something called fate, something called destiny. Fate brought us together. It was predestined.

As the fire devoured the house, a single shadow crept away into the darkness.

The murder of the Cummings weighed heavy on the hearts and minds of the nation. No one could remember a crime of such brutality, such cruelty. The nation was baffled. How could a nation of quiet, peaceful, fete loving people give rise to such monsters? This was a crime of big countries, not a twenty-one by fourteen mile, sleepy, banana island, not a country of one season. The nation was baffled. What were monsters doing in their midst?

These same thoughts occupied the minds of Keith, Vernon,

and Mitchell, as they sat at the Green Parrot Restaurant and Bar, two Saturdays since the night of death by fire. For a while they sat quietly. Then Keith gave voice to what dwelt on their minds.

"Did you know how the police found him out? The police owe me a big favor. Let me tell you how they got him. The Wednesday following the murder, Sylvia, one of the cashiers working for me, came to work wearing a gold chain. The chain caught my eye because it resembled one of the chains Lynne used to wear. So I examined the chain more closely, telling Sylvia how nice the chain looked, and the man that gave it to her must really be in love with her. At the back of the heart shaped locket was the initial, "L.C." I knew then the chain belonged to Lynne. I asked Sylvia who gave her the chain, who was her boyfriend. She smiled and said 'you jealous.' I told her I wasn't, but that I would like to know where I could buy a chain like that for my wife. She said, 'my boyfriend said he bought it from a man that just came from Guyana with a lot of gold.' Good, I said, I must speak to your boyfriend to find the whereabouts of this man from Guyana. 'His name is Robert and he lives in the Conway. I will tell him you want to see him, maybe he can come by tomorrow,' she replied

"I didn't wait for tomorrow. Shortly after I spoke with Sylvia, I went to the police. They came right away to the store. As soon as the police began to question Sylvia, she started blabbering non-stop. 'I didn't steal anything. There is nothing wrong in accepting a gift. People had warned me about that Robert. People said he hurts women, and he is a crook. I was avoiding him for a whole month, but when he gave me the chain, I said to myself, that man loves me.' The police listened patiently to Sylvia, and when she had run out of gas, they asked her where they could find Robert.

"This was how they caught the murderer. The two Scotland Yard agents that came down to help the investigation had nothing to do with it. The police owe me a medal. They should make me Chief of Police."

There was a silence. The men took turns shaking their heads.

It was hard for this monstrous event, this unfathomable thing, to seep in. Keith related the story, but he too was shaking his head.

"You know," said Keith, "what beats me is why them? Why out of all people he had to pick the Cummings? Not too long ago Anthony was telling me how his great-great grandfather fought on the side of freedom in the American War of Independence, and how his father was a general in World War I. Anthony himself volunteered for World War II. Both he and Lynne were actively involved in the Civil Rights movement. They marched with Martin Luther King, supported the black panthers, and were paying members of the NAACP. Right here in St. Lucia, they were always making donations to sport clubs and to the boy scouts. They donated half of their library to the Convent. I don't know what this country is coming to. There is a laziness, a don't carishness sweeping this country. Nobody wants to work. All they want to do is smoke dope, steal, and loot. Mark my words. This country is going down the drain, this is just the beginning."

"Keith, it's a real shame what happened to Anthony and Lynne," said Mitchell. " I was just as shocked as everybody else. The murderer deserves nothing less than the gallows. But you should also realize that the government needs to do more for the youth of this country. Many of our youths have to be turned away from secondary school because there isn't enough space. Jobs are almost non-existent, children go to bed hungry. The government needs to pay more attention to the poor of this country. Or else the masses will soon erupt, and once the fireball starts rolling there is no stopping it. It will burn and destroy everything in its path."

"Mitchell, I agree with you one hundred percent," said Vernon. "No one is more sorry about the murder of Anthony and Lynne than I am. After all, just a month ago they were coaxing me to accompany them on their next trip to the States. But you are right. And as I have always said, the UWP is a party of the rich. Well, the masses are growling. The UWP better listen. Because how much longer the masses will wait, no one knows."

192

"You all guys disgust me," said Keith. "Our friends have been brutally murdered, for no-good reason, and instead of putting the blame where it belongs, you all guys are blaming the government. That is exactly what is wrong with this country. People like you are not holding our youth responsible for their own actions. Someone rapes and robs a tourist, we blame the government; people abandon school, they don't look for work, instead they watch the business of the streets day and night, but when they go hungry, we blame the government. A vagabond who has never done an honest day's work murdered our friends, we blame the government. Trust you guys to turn everything into a political football. Guys, this is no game. For no reason under the sun, a wharf-rat invaded the homes of two innocent people, and burned them to ashes. This isn't a game. This is murder, murder in the extreme. Until we start holding our youth responsible for their own actions, this is just the start of social and cultural disintegration. You all disgust me. I have no time for this crap." That said, Keith walked out of the Green Parrot.

As he walked out, the gods of the land laughed at the folly of men.

But unlike the gods of the land, the people of Conway weren't laughing. This was no laughing matter. In times like this, only demons and gods could afford to laugh. The Conway was already known for its poverty, its lawlessness, its vulgarity, but now it was clear to the rest of Castries, to the rest of the country, that Conway people were cursed. Ras Gimie, a rastafarian of high standing in Castries, prophesied that it wouldn't be long before Conway was wiped off the face of the earth. Even so, Like the rest of the nation, the murders shocked the people of Conway.

Colletta, the only person who would not have been shocked nor surprised was two years dead. When the news arrived of whom the murderer was, Colletta's closest neighbors, Sophia, Cora and Lydia sought each other's company to fathom the unfathomable. They gathered in the cool of the late afternoon at Cora's doorsteps, in front of a noisy group of boys pitching marbles.

Speaking above the noise of the boys, Sophia said, "my God! My God! You mean to tell me the people didn't do the boy anything, yet he murder the people like that? Burn the people alive. The people were just there minding their own business. I knew Conway people were bad, but this, this wickedness is too much, is beyond my comprehension."

"We are at the end of times," said Cora. "This world has gotten too wicked. In the last days the wicked will harden up their hearts. All the signs of Christ's second coming are here. It will not be long before the Messiah returns and bring this wickedness to an end."

"You see that," said Lydia, "all the time Colletta was saying that the boy Robert was cursed and would end in jail or the gallows, we didn't pay her any mind, but she was right after all."

"Despite Colletta's misgivings," said Cora, " I was hoping that God would have laid his hands on the boy and turn him around, point him in the right direction."

"I don't know, Cora," said Sophia, "this abomination proves that some people are beyond the reach of God."

"Don't say that, Sophia, it is never too late to repent," said Cora. "Even now the boy has a chance to repent of his sins and ask God's forgiveness. Even now he still has a chance to enter the Kingdom of God. Remember the man that was crucified with Christ, the one who said *Lord, remember me when thou comest into thy Kingdom.* And Jesus said to him *Verily I say unto thee, today shalt thou be with me in paradise.*"

"Give me a break. You are carrying this religion thing too far," said Sophia. "After what the boy did, you are still talking about him entering the Kingdom of God. The boy should burn in hell. End of story."

"Sophia, don't underestimate the mercy of God," said Cora. "He said: *Though your sins (they) be red like crimson, they shall be as wool.*"

"When I heard Felina's boy was the one who did it,"said
Lydia, "I was half expecting to hear that Christine's boy was in
on it too. After all, he kept following Felina's boy as if the boy
was his shadow."

"Yeah, I thought the same thing too", said Sophia.

"Me too," said Cora.

"That's why I always used to tell my children to be careful
who their friends are," said Sophia. "Show me your friends, I will
tell you who you are."

"It always baffled me what Christine's boy saw in Felina's
boy," said Lydia.

"You know," said Sophia, "I heard they were man and wife,
they slept with each other."

"What an abomination!" said Cora. "Sodom and Gomorrah
all over again, we are in the last days."

He was in jail wondering how he had gotten himself in this
situation. He hated no one. He never had a desire to hurt people.
So how did he find himself in this situation? He examined his life
to see where he went wrong. The events of the past rolled on like
a movie. Stealing Shirley biscuits at M&C, stealing ripe bananas
up the Morne, stealing Colletta's money, repeatedly raping Rosa,
and on and on the list went. Always, his shadow was with him,
coaxing, prodding, compelling him to come along. My God, he
thought, how did I allow him to do that to me. Damn, Damn,
Damn. I am the worse ass in the world. Now I am going to pay
for it. Why didn't I listen to the voice inside me that always told
me this was wrong? Why, why, why? He thought about Christine.
Oh how much he missed her. It occurred to him that he had spent
all of his life missing and looking for his mother, all of his life long-
ing for her. He sobbed violently. But the film continued to roll.
Night went away and morning brought two policemen. They supported him as he walked weakly to his execution. He kept his gaze
down and never looked at the crowd. He was so weak that the

policemen had to just about lift him up the steps to the hanging platform. As they guided him under the gallows, he wet himself without realizing it. He glanced at the crowd and saw eyes filled with pity. "Such a good-looking boy," he heard them saying. "It is that other boy who has led him to the gallows. Did you know he is the son of that woman? Christine, yes Christine? The one who won the Carnival Queen way back and died in the accident not too long ago? Now that was a beautiful woman." As the policeman tightened the noose around his neck, he closed his eyes tight. And it was then that he saw the face of Christine rising above the Pitons, and Christine grew into a giant, and she stood on top of the Pitons, her right foot on Gros Piton and the left on Petit Piton. And he was standing at the foot of the pitons, between the pitons, and Christine bent down, stretched out her hands, picked him up, and held him to her bosom, and he gazed with wonder and then with weeping eyes over the beauty of the island and its surrounding waters. He wept because this was the first time he had realized how beautiful his country was, yet this would be the last time he would see such beauty.

With this thought, Trevor opened his eyes to find out he wasn't in jail at all, but in his bed, and the execution tomorrow wasn't his, but Robert's. Trevor wept. He wept for the joy of being able to see the beauty of the land as often as he wished and he wept with the sorrow that tomorrow his shadow would be no more.

A large crowd gathered to witness the hanging. It was ten o'clock in the morning, and a gentle breeze was blowing across Castries. The sky was clear and the sun was already shining brightly. Two policemen flanked Robert. His hands tied behind his back. The policemen gently directed him under the noose, onto the trap door. Once there, Robert looked at the crowd. He had a slight grin on his face, as if he were amused that so many people had come to pay their respects. He saw Trevor, and the silly grin on his face turned to a smile of recognition. He was glad he had made good by his friend. After the night of death by fire, Trevor had wanted to put him out, saying he wanted nothing to do with him, and he wanted no part of what happened up the Morne. He had assured Trevor that no one would find out, he had burned all the evidence. Besides if they found out, he would make sure that they knew that Trevor had nothing to do with it, that it was all his doing. Despite what was to come, it was reassuring to know that right to the end he had done right by his friend, the only human being (the only living creature, for that matter) that he had truly been able to make contact with. His eyes then left the face of Trevor and the other faces of the crowd. He saw the rays of the sun. He noted that today would be a beautiful day. The policeman placed the noose around his neck, and tightened it a bit. The noose felt comfortable around his neck, as if it had been there all his life. His countenance was calm and peaceful. He suddenly felt relieved. He felt like a man who was born to a mission and the mission was now accomplished. He looked at the crowd again, his brother, Ralph, home on summer vacation, was there but Robert had no eyes for him, instead his eyes picked up rum-reeking Rosa. He smiled at her. She shuddered. She felt like she knew him. The scent of moist earth and decaying leaves mixed with perfume filled her nostrils and she felt a sharp pain. At that very moment the trap door came to life and Rosa wasn't sure whether it was her pain she felt or that of Robert's.

Anderson Reynolds was born and raised in Vieux Fort, St. Lucia. He holds a doctorate degree in Food and Resource Economics from the University of Florida. He resides in St. Lucia and is currently preparing a volume of his poetry for publication.